The wolf moved again, slinking to one side so that Shiva was forced toward a gap between two rocks. This must be where the wolves wished to herd her; and if they succeeded, she would be dead in minutes.

There was only one possible course of action, and she took it. With a howl of fury, Shiva threw herself upon the wolf. . . .

She struggled for the knife, knowing it could not save her. This time there was no escape. She fell in a confusion of wolf smell and wolf breath and snarling and fangs. Then the wolf screamed and jerked away from her.

Instinctively, Shiva rolled, heedless of the pain the movement brought. She jumped to her feet, wondering if she could possibly attempt to run, then froze.

There was a boy astride the wolf.

SHIVA

AN ADVENTURE
OF THE ICE AGE

J. H. BRENNAN

CONSULTANT, JOYCE POPE

HarperTrophy
A Division of HarperCollinsPublishers

Shiva: An Adventure of the Ice Age
Copyright © 1989 by J. H. Brennan
First published in England by William Collins Sons & Co. Ltd, 8 Grafton
Street, London.

First American Edition, 1990.

Library of Congress Cataloging-in-Publication Data
Brennan, J. H.
  Shiva: an adventure of the Ice Age / J. H. Brennan :
consultant, Joyce Pope.
      p.   cm.
  Summary: A Cro-Magnon tribe is forced to confront its collective fear
of the Neanderthal people they call ogres, when a young girl of the
tribe, Shiva, befriends an ogre boy, and when Hiram, a young hunter
from the tribe, is captured by the ogres.
  ISBN 0-397-32453-7. — ISBN 0-397-32454-5 (lib. bdg.)
  ISBN 0-06-440392-0 (pbk.)
  [1. Man, Prehistoric—Fiction.]   I. Pope, Joyce.   II. Title.
PZ7.B75155Sh   1990   89-11654
[Fic]—dc20   CIP
                                                               AC

First Harper Trophy edition, 1992.
Manufactured in the United Kingdom by HarperCollins.

*For Murray
who thought of the
idea and Gail
who liked it.*

Contents

1
Shiva Hunted

There was something stalking her.

Shiva stopped, nostrils twitching. The briefest of wind changes had carried the musty, feral scent, so fleeting it might have been imagination.

She turned slowly, full circle, attempting to discover the source of that chilling odor. Her eyes moved cautiously across the rocky outcrops, across the shrub and the scrub and the stunted, twisted trees that had given her the wood she now carried.

Nothing . . .

She bobbed her head, as the great cats did, tempting the predator to stand out and be seen. Still nothing. But there were a hundred hiding places.

It was a wolf smell.

The packs were forest hunters, ready to attack

1

anything foolish enough to enter their domain. But occasionally they ranged farther. And though they seldom troubled humans, it sometimes happened that they took an unwary child.

Could she reach the safety of the shelters before the wolf attacked?

Or should she call for help now? They would hear. She was certain they would hear. But her call might provoke the wolf to attack at once. If it did, any help would certainly arrive too late.

Shiva looked around for a tree she could climb or a rock she could scale. Then she could call from safety, and the hunters would come and drive away the wolf.

There was a tree, taller than most here, but could she reach it? Where was the wolf? She prayed to the Great Mother Goddess for another change of wind to carry the scent that would tell her where the danger lay.

But the Great Mother had turned her face from Shiva. The wind remained stubbornly from the south and carried only scents of resin and fern.

For some reason she found herself thinking of all the suffering her tribe had lately endured. First there was Momo, a hunter who had died of the purple death after the setting of a full moon . . . then there were the two other hunters who were maimed by tawny cats and later died . . . and there was a child who died after a fall. The unexplained death of an old woman had also hit the tribe hard, especially because she was the grandmother of Renka, the woman who led the tribe. Even the changing season and the move to the spring camp had not banished misfortune from the tribe.

Would Shiva be the next to go?

She began to move, edging her way cautiously in the direction of the tree. A short-haired, bright-eyed girl, her brown skin was burned by wind and weather. Her body, arms and legs were mostly hidden by the skins she wore, rough cut and still smelling of animal, but her knees were bare. Shiva had seen less than fifty seasons: She was eleven, perhaps twelve, years old.

She was an orphan of the tribe.

She carried her bone club in her left hand, the hand she had favored since birth. The *ogre hand* the old ones called it, and they looked on her with suspicion because of that . . . and other things. She disliked being considered odd and sometimes prayed to the Great Mother to make her more like the others.

Suddenly the wind changed and Shiva's nostrils were filled with the sour smell of wolf. It was close by. And something else, less familiar, more disturbing. Shiva ran toward the tree. The wolf stepped out at once.

Shiva stopped and dropped into a crouch, brandishing the useless bone club. The wolf was neither young nor overlarge, a graying bitch with yellow eyes; and all the more dangerous for her years of experience. She snarled, eyeing Shiva threateningly.

Shiva waited, still wondering if she should risk a call. There was no possibility of reaching the tree now and never any real possibility of outrunning the wolf once it had seen her. So she had only one option: to stand and fight.

The wolf moved forward and Shiva backed away. She knew now she would soon be dead, but strangely the thought did not disturb her. Shiva almost looked forward to it; she had never known her mother.

The wolf moved again, slinking to one side so that Shiva was forced toward a gap between two rocks. Something in the wolf's deliberation made Shiva think of the way the hunters sometimes herded prey. Was she too being herded? If so, there were two wolves, not one. Where was the second? Lurking hidden in the shelter of the rocks? Almost certainly.

When Shiva stopped, the wolf made a small, darting movement toward her, snarling. Although her heart pounded in her chest, she held her ground and the wolf swerved away, but circled so that it was facing her again.

4

What to do now?

Shiva glanced around. The wolf remained between her and the tree. There were no rocks close at hand so sheer the wolf could not follow her up them. To call out now would be to invite an immediate attack, that was certain.

What to do?

Behind her and a little to the right, she caught the same sound she had heard earlier, like the clink of a dislodged pebble. Which meant the second wolf was there, still in hiding, but growing restless. How long before it too showed itself and both animals attacked?

She risked a quick glance behind her. The gap between the two rocks led through to a natural enclosure from which it seemed there was no exit. This must be where the wolves wished to herd her; and if they succeeded, she would be dead in minutes.

At the same time, if she waited too long and the second wolf emerged from hiding, the same fate awaited. However fiercely she fought, however swiftly she ran, she was no match for two full-grown wolves.

There was only one possible course of action, and she took it. With a howl of fury, Shiva threw herself upon the wolf.

2
Bite of Death

Shiva struck with the club aiming at the base of the skull, hoping to kill it or to stun it or, if she missed, to catch the neck and perhaps wound it severely. But the wolf twisted so that her blow went wild, grazing its shoulder without drawing blood.

But her attack, so unexpected, startled the beast, and it did not attempt to savage her, but rather tried to flee, stumbling over its own feet in the process. Then it swung around and came at her again, leaping for her throat.

Shiva dropped to her knees, ducking to one side so the momentum of the wolf carried it across her shoulder, so close the fur of its hide brushed her cheek and the claws of one forepaw raked her neck painfully, but without drawing blood. She tried to keep her balance, failed and fell forward. She rolled with the movement and sprang to her feet, turning to find the wolf leaping at her again.

This time it caught her full in the chest and she went down heavily, striking at the wolf's flanks with her club repeatedly. She twisted her head away as the wolf sought her throat, her nostrils full of wolf smell.

Incredibly, it missed her throat, but gripped her ear, tearing away part of the lobe. There was no pain, none. She wriggled, finding herself under the wolf, her mouth half filled with the fur of its stomach. She twisted onto hands and knees, scarcely knowing what she was doing, and the weight of the wolf left her.

As she tried to climb to her feet again, it struck her violently from the side, throwing her across a rock. She struck her head and felt darkness surrounding her.

Shiva rolled sideways from the rock, unsteadily regaining her feet. Her head throbbed, her back felt sore and bruised. Beneath the sticky wetness of her blood, there was an ache in her ear that spread down through her neck. Worse, she had struck her left shoulder, weakening the arm; and she no longer held the club.

Right-handed now, she struggled for the knife,

knowing it could not save her. The gray shape circled, holding its distance momentarily, then sprang. Shiva jerked the knife up, hoping to catch its belly, then went down again beneath the charge. This time there was no escape. She fell in a confusion of wolf smell and wolf breath and snarling and fangs. Then the wolf screamed and jerked away from her.

Instinctively, Shiva rolled, heedless of the pain the movement brought. She jumped to her feet, wondering if she could possibly attempt to run, then froze.

There was a boy astride the wolf.

Nothing—nothing of importance—ever happens by accident, the Crone's voice whispered in her mind.

He was the strangest boy she had ever seen, smaller than she in height, though stocky and far more heavily muscled. His hair was very long and black, and though he seemed young, he had a covering of fine body hair, almost like a downy fur. Beneath the body hair she could see his skin coloring was much darker than her own—or much more dirty. His head was large and misshapen, with a heavy, chinless jaw, a monstrous bony ridge above both eyes and a bulge at the back of his skull. One arm was locked around the wolf's throat, the other held her club.

But the boy was not using the club to attack. Instead, he had fastened his teeth in the back of the wolf's neck and was clinging like a great cat when it brings down a horse.

The wolf screamed again, a chilling, fearsome sound, then convulsed and collapsed. The boy rolled off in a single fluid movement that took him onto large flat feet. As Shiva watched, he approached the wolf and began to beat it experimentally about the head and back with her club. It made no movement, obviously dead. The boy's expression changed and he jumped up and down in what could have been excitement or a victory dance. He ran around the body several times, moving very quickly, but with a stooped, loping gait. Then he stopped and sniffed the air and turned toward her.

Shiva had never seen a boy so strange. His nostrils were flat and broad, like those of a beast. Even at rest, his face looked angry. He was not of the tribe and smelled rank. Nonetheless, he had killed the wolf.

She waited, unsure what to do. The boy turned and kicked the body a few times, fell to examining her old bone club minutely, then dropped it on the ground. He moved toward her nervously, still sniffing.

Shiva stood very still, hardly aware of the throbbing in her ear.

He circled her curiously, moved closer, backed off, flat nostrils twitching, then reached out to finger an edge of the skins she wore. Shiva watched, fascinated. This was the second scent, the second noise: not a second wolf, but this strange boy who had killed the wolf. Eventually, when she sensed the worst of his nervousness had died, she said, "Who are you, boy? I am Shiva."

He leaped back as if he had been stung, and for an instant she was sure he would flee. But he held his ground, watching her intently with huge brown eyes. Now that she had become a little accustomed to his strange looks, she thought his eyes at least were beautiful, like those of aurochs cattle—soft and liquid.

"Who are you, boy?" she repeated.

He made no sound but looked at her, tilting his head to one side. Then, as if bored, he shuffled back to the body of the wolf and circled it again. He glanced at her, then went into the curious flat-footed jumping dance she had witnessed earlier.

Some part of his thoughts communicated with her so that she nodded. "Yes, you killed it." He came toward her again, less nervously this time, and squatted no more than three paces away, watching her.

Shiva retrieved her club, finding it so battered now that it was scarcely usable. She tucked it into her belt and moved to the wolf, for while it was his kill, he seemed too young to know what to do, and it was easier to skin any animal when the flesh was still warm.

He watched her with consuming interest as she used her flint knife to make a ring cut on the back legs, just above the knee. She inspected her work, then did the same on the forelegs. She cut down the inside of the rear legs and cut in a long, slow sweep along the belly, using two fingers inserted behind the blade to lift the skin. Finally she cut along the inside of the forelegs.

Working more quickly now, she removed the scent glands under the tail, for she had been taught that these would taint the meat if left intact. She eased the skin of the hind legs away from the flesh using her knife as little as possible, then rolled it outward, the fur inside itself, and pulled it down.

She had to cut a circle around the wolf's tail before easing the skin from the back, but once that was done, it came away easily enough, and in a single, untorn piece. She was pleased. Wolfskin was warm and much prized, and the women would praise her, although she would not be allowed to keep it.

Still watched by the strange boy, she dragged the

carcass out of the forbidden rocks and left it on a piece of open ground, knowing that men would be sent to fetch it when she appeared with the skin. She looked toward the cliff and the camp, noticing a small plume of smoke from a fire. Now that the danger was past, she felt a tingle of warm anticipation. Safety was so close.

The strange-looking boy had shuffled beside her and was fingering her clothing again. He had still not said a word, and she wondered if his mind was slow. She found the minds of many other children slow compared with her own—often children older than herself and even adults, too. Certainly a normal boy would have protested when she skinned his wolf.

She started toward the camp and he followed, pausing when she paused, moving when she moved.

She wondered what to do about him. He was not of her tribe.

3

Memories of a Magic Grove

Hiram was of Shiva's tribe and Hiram was afraid.

He squatted near the entrance of the longhouse, absently searching the leaf carpet for a succulent grub or beetle. From time to time his eyes were drawn to the narrow passageway, dimly illuminated by flickering firelight from the inner chamber. He wore the tawny girdle of a hunter, but even that was no protection from his fear.

Women always frightened him. Even girls his own age made him uneasy, for they were full of secrets they would not share. But when it came to the Council of the Elder Women, his unease transformed itself into downright terror. No elder woman had ever spoken sharply to Hiram, for he was an obedient youth and a skillful hunter, but still he feared them. His eyes flickered to the passageway and back.

A young woman entered, carrying a wooden bowl with such care he knew it must be brimming. He had noticed her before, for she was dark and pretty, although he did not know her name. She glanced at him and smiled, as girls often did. Hiram flushed and looked down quickly at the floor. When he gathered enough courage to look up again, she was gone. He knew she must have taken the passage to the inner chamber, perhaps bringing some witch brew to the elders.

Why, he wondered, did it have to be him?

He could not imagine they would believe him. They might listen to his story—they were very good at listening. But they were also very good at remembering and they would not believe him. They would not believe him because they would remember the shameful business of the marula grove. Hiram thought back. . . .

Two summers before, when the tribe ranged far to the south, Hiram, a novice hunter then, his tawny skin belt earned only a few moons earlier, chanced upon a hippopotamus that had done a thing so strange that it was almost wondrous. It had left its river home by day.

Hiram saw it and froze in disbelief, then tracked it, wondering.

14

The hippo moved without caution or fear, head high, eyes glittering, obviously following a defined route. It did not stop. It did not pause. It did not hesitate. And not once did it graze.

Hiram was forced to drop into the familiar hunter's trot in order to keep up. He caught the glint of water before its scent reached him, a shallow pool, which the hippo ignored.

In the pool, staring intently at its own reflection, was a Lightning Bird.

Hiram's excitement had peaked. Even at the risk of losing his prey, he halted briefly and knelt and touched his head respectfully to the ground while facing in the Lightning Bird's direction. The white, long-legged wader was the most magical of all flying creatures. That such a bird should appear at just this time was an omen for sure.

Squatting by the longhouse now, Hiram thought back to that time and wondered how he could have been so wrong. Everybody knew the Lightning Bird was a very special omen. And yet, on that occasion, it had pointed him toward the disaster. Maybe his mistake had been going alone. Had he happened to have Shiva with him, she might even have been able to explain the Lightning Bird.

But he had had no one with him. He had been

alone then as he was now. He glanced toward the dark interior of the longhouse, wondering how long it would be before the women sent for him. He shivered and let his mind drift back to that day.

He soon caught up with the hippo, but stayed a safe distance behind so that it would not see him.

In time they had come to a marula grove.

Although he had never before seen a marula, Hiram knew at once what he had found. The elegant trees, with their graceful leaves, were spoken of again and again in the histories of the tribe—and figured frequently in tribal lore.

Hiram stared in wonder. The marula fruit was a gift of the Mother Goddess herself, a fruit so special there was none other like it. Far to the south, where legend said the tribe was born, there were many marula—but here in the colder northlands, where the tribe had wandered generations past to escape a time of barrenness and drought, the marula was rare. Many, like Hiram, had never seen one and knew it only by its legend and its reputation as a bringer of joy, to humans and animals alike.

Hiram had listened to the fireside tales of the marula, believing, yet not believing. He was astounded by the descriptions of the southern lands

16

where the weather was so warm there was no need
to wear skins at any time of year; astounded by
the story that the Mother actually came down to
earth to tread the marula fruit.

But these were tales of long ago and far away,
and he had never thought he would see marula
in the cold north, although some of the elders
claimed a strain of the tree did grow here and bore
fruit in the brief summer.

The elders.

His eyes were drawn back to the longhouse, and one hand reached out to scratch nervously at a small sore above his ankle. He was absolutely certain they were not going to believe him. Not the elder women, not his fellow hunters, not anyone.

Shiva might believe you, his mind contradicted him at once. But he dismissed the thought. Shiva might believe because she was his secret friend, but Shiva was hardly more than a child, and known to be strange. No one *else* would believe him now because of that accursed marula grove. He had been so certain of what he had seen.

He knew he was looking at marula. For an instant
he even wondered if he would see the Mother God-
dess too, come to trample the fruit. The hippo trot-

17

ted directly to the mushy golden carpet and began at once to eat, shoveling prodigious quantities of the fruit into its mouth. Hiram stared. Never had he seen a hippo eat anything but grass.

It seemed that all creation had found the grove. There were many, many creatures here besides the newly arrived hippo. He noticed a group of sows with their attendant boar, four hyenas, several large rodents, a handful of giant shrews, one or two deer and a multitude of birds. None took fright as he approached and none bothered to threaten him. The Mother's peace was upon them, as told in the old tales. All the same, he gave a wide berth to the boar, a notoriously dangerous and bad-tempered animal.

He made a cup of his hands, scooped some mush from the ground and half ate, half drank it down.

To his amazement it burned on his tongue, and in his throat. It burned a track down the inside of his body to his stomach, where it caught fire and began to glow. Hiram licked his lips. The flavor was pleasant, but more so was the magic fire hidden in the pulp. He scooped more and drank that too.

In half an hour, Hiram was propped against the tree, no longer caring if the boar gutted him. He was experiencing joy and the Mother's peace.

He felt warm and relaxed and a little sick. The simplest things amused him hugely. He laughed at the progress of a beetle on the tree bark, and even began to sing the tribal night songs, but he could not quite hold the rhythm. His lips and the tip of his nose were numb: He kept biting his lips to make sure they were still there. His vision blurred frequently and sometimes he saw double, so that there were two hippos lying on their backs in the mush. When he tried to stand, he staggered, feeling his body heavy as stone.

Remembering, he wished he could recapture something of that feeling at this moment. But now, waiting for his summons, there was only a dry mouth and nervousness and fear. He hoped the elders would summon him soon, for the longer he waited, the more fearful he felt. How different now from the way it had been then. . . .

Despite the fog that threatened to enclose his mind, he knew what he must do. He must tell the tribe. He must tell the tribe and lead them to the grove.

Hiram staggered far from the sacred grove, unable to find his path and scarcely caring. Eventually he fell into a deep, dreamless sleep.

He awoke with the dawn so ill, he knew at once

he must be close to death. His head pounded with pain, and the sour-sweet taste in his mouth was converted into dust. His body trembled, and when he moved he experienced such weakness that it seemed he could not possibly go on. He groaned aloud, shivering, and forced himself to stand. Nothing near him looked familiar.

Eventually he stumbled on a game trail, which took him to a stream. He felt much better after drinking the cold water, so much so that, before the sun had set, he had found his way back to the encampment of the tribe.

Despite his tiredness and the dull pounding in his head, he entered the camp with joy, the hunter who had found the sacred grove. Was he not the stuff of legend now, because of his discovery? Would his name not live forever?

That night, around the fires, he told everyone of his discovery. The tribe listened wide-eyed, the elders with a little more reserve.

The following morning Hiram led the tribe in search of the marula grove. He led them for that day and half the next but could not find the grove.

He would never forget the humiliation of that second day, never forget the taunts of the children, the glares of his fellow hunters, the quiet, penetrating witch stares of the women. He would never forget the disbelief, the growing panic, the desperation, the loss of face. There was no punishment, although he remained in terror of the possibility it would one day prevent his becoming Keeper of the Sacred Drums. But he knew his tribe would never forget either.

The dark, pretty girl emerged from the narrow passageway and smiled at him again. She nodded and gestured, so he knew the elder council was ready to receive him.

Drawing his courage about him like a cloak, Hiram rose and shuffled through the passage to the inner chamber. It was a place of totems, skulls and bones, herbs hung drying, heat and the heavy smell of witchcraft everywhere. The women looked at him expectantly, their faces made strange by the firelight; none stranger than the Crone in the soothsayer's niche nearest the fire.

Hiram swallowed, dropped his eyes and muttered his news.

"We cannot hear you, hunter," Renka called at once, not unkindly. Her eyes bored into him. She was the leader of the tribe. "Speak clearly and do not be afraid."

He spoke clearly then, although he remained desperately afraid. "Elders," he said, "I have seen an ogre clan."

4

The Missing Child

Far from the longhouse and the village camp were caverns hidden in the depths of the forest. None from Shiva's tribe would have dared to enter, yet inside there squatted a monstrous figure, lost in gloom and thought.

His thoughts were strange in form—few words and many pictures. His features were flat, his skull misshapen. His jaw was heavy, his brow ridged. He was huge, strong and ugly.

He thought of spring.

With spring came new rivers, marshes, swamps. The meltwaters of the great ice flowed faster than the earth could drink them.

It was a time of danger. The clan had once found the broken body of a furred rhinoceros smashed against rocks at the bend of a riverbed that had been dry an hour before. They had watched a

22

mammoth sucked down by the spring swamp, its huge strength useless against the swamp's grip.

Thag found himself remembering such things although he had no wish to. For if the woolly rhino and the mammoth died so easily, might not . . . a person . . . have died too? Might not his missing son Doban have died too? Here, on a high ledge, in the depths of the caverns, he could face the truth at last. His son was gone. *Perhaps* was dead . . .

Idly he scratched his belly, forcing his mind to create different, less disturbing thoughts. He was squatting on a high ledge, partly concealed in a natural rock niche, the better to hide from Hana. He was a creature of enormous proportions, the strongest by far in the clan, hence its natural leader. His courage was unquestioned—he had once torn apart a cat that threatened a child. But for all that, he was terrified of Hana's tongue. She would want him to search again for their son, as if he had not already searched. As if there were anywhere left to search. Did she not know the vastness of the forest? Did she not know the reach of the river? *Did she not know the tundra stretched forever?* Thag growled deep in his throat, angry with Hana. She was a stupid, *stupid* woman, knowing nothing. Had he not searched *everywhere* for Doban—then searched again?

The anger made him feel a little better. He curled

one huge hand into a fist and thumped the rock beside his feet, mindless of the pain. She had no sense of his position! *None!*

The vivid pictures formed within Thag's head, so strongly he could step inside them.

He was seated on the Rock of Judgment, he, Thag, chief of the clan. On his left hand Hagar, all but toothless now, yet full of wisdom. And before them, bound, the creature Shil, who had stolen Heft the Hunter's meat. Thag was angry with Shil, for the stealing of another's meat was a great crime—except meat from a different clan, of course, when theft was a duty.

"It was not me!" Shil shouted. He was almost as big as Thag, and had twice tried—unsuccessfully—to wrench the leadership from him.

"It was you!" Thag shouted back, pounding the Rock of Judgment. "Meat stealer! Pigface!"

Shil snapped his bonds, which were in any case no more than ceremonial, creeping vines wrapped around his arms and upper body, scarcely strong enough to hold a newborn baby. He jumped forward so that his face was close to Thag's own, teeth bared. "Pigface yourself, Thag! Who can show I stole the meat? Did Heft see me? Did any see me?"

24

"He has a point there," Hagar whispered.

"Pebblebrain!" Thag growled, baring his own strong teeth.

He took a deep breath, threw back his own head and howled, "Stealer of Heft's meat!"

There was a murmur of interest from those gathered in the cave, for now a fight seemed certain. It had been a long time since Thag had fought with Shil, and there were some who thought the outcome might not be a foregone conclusion.

"Dung eater!" hissed Shil, delivering the ultimate insult. He reached out and insolently curled the hair upon Thag's chest around his little finger.

At which point—at which point in these solemn deliberations—Hana had chosen to interrupt.

Thag could scarcely believe it. The administration of justice was man's work. Women were forbidden to enter the judgment hall by long and hallowed tradition. The clan was ruled by men. The laws were made by men. And men were judged by men. Yet here she was before him, emerging out of nowhere like the memory of a horrid dream.

"He has gone!" she told him bluntly. She pushed Shil, taller than she by a head and a half and twice her bulk. He stumbled and turned on her with a savage growl. But she glared at him and he retreated, muttering. Then she turned her

25

attention back to Thag. *"Doban has gone,"* she repeated grimly, *"and it is* your *fault!"*

His fault? *His* fault? Even now the memory of her words was enough to make his stomach knot, causing bitter bile to well up in his throat. . . .

"My fault?" he growled, appalled. *She had come here, disrupting his court, and she was accusing him before the whole assembled clan. The whole* male *part of the clan, he corrected himself, which was the only part that mattered.* And the only part allowed to stand before the Rock of Judgment! *he screamed at her in his mind.*

She was tiny. And did not know her place. Her hair was white or perhaps yellow. In any case, unlike the hair of any other. His own hair was black, where it had not turned gray. And he was strong. By all the gods he was strong! The strongest of the clan! How could he have taken her for a mate? She trod on custom, shamed him before the clan. He glared at her. She would apologize at once for her disruption of a court of justice. Then she would leave. "You will leave this cave at once!" *he roared.*

"Well," she asked sharply, *"will you not search for him* now?"

26

She was not leaving. She never did what he told her. However much he instructed her, she never did. Why did she not obey? He was strong, the strongest of the clan.

He knew of whom she spoke. They had talked of nothing else that morning before his duties called him to the Rock of Judgment. The boy, Thag told her, was with his aunt Mara. Or his friends. Or chasing after squirrels in the manner of boys. "Find him yourself," he told her. "I have more important things to do." As he had. Was he not chief?

"I went to Mara. He is not with her," Hana shouted. "I went to the caves of his friends. They have not seen him."

Thag chilled. Earlier, when she had told him, he had thought the boy was with Mara. He had to be with Mara, with Mara or with his friends, for if he was not, then he was . . . Thag stopped the thought.

"Does she speak of Doban?" Hagar whispered.

Thag ignored him. "All his friends?" he asked her. Doban had many friends. "Every one? Go to all his friends, woman." He noticed that the men congregated within the chamber of justice had drawn closer, the better to see and hear.

"Have you bone between your ears?" Hana

27

asked him fiercely. *"I have told you he is not within the dwellings of the clan. Not, you great aurochs! Not!* Not! *You must search for him beyond. You and your hunters. Use your men's skills and search. And find him. Do it now!"*

Heads turned from Hana toward Thag.

Thag found he did not wish to search. To search would mean the boy was truly gone. If he had left the dwellings of the clan, then he was dead. Could she not understand that if they admitted the boy Doban had left the sheltered caverns of the clan, then he was embraced by bear or eaten by cat or taken by the swamp? Thag did not wish such things to have happened. He loved Doban. He would never admit Doban was missing from the caverns of the clan. He would not search!

He swung down from the Rock of Judgment, swept out his strong left arm to brush aside those fools who had ventured too close. "I will search!" he hissed. *"You hear me, woman? I will search at once! I, Thag, will find Doban!* Stupid woman!"

"Do it quickly," Hana said.

Do it quickly. Do it quickly. The words echoed through his head as he squatted on the high ledge. There was a sickness in his stomach, a sickness born of emptiness. Death was all around. Every clan family knew death, but some deaths left an emptiness that would not be filled.

Do it quickly. As if he would waste a moment. He stared into the pictures created by his mind and saw himself sweep out of the cave, bowling over those who stood in his path, leaving Shil unpunished.

Thag and Heft the Hunter, Thonar, Kral, Mabango, Dan, the greatest, strongest, most skilled, most cunning of the clan, had left the caverns then and searched for Doban in the forest, then beyond the forest. They searched in the rocks and by the river, and where the ice wind blew. They searched throughout the entire *world* avoiding only the encampment of the Weakling Strangers and their cunning spears.

If such men as these could not find Doban, then . . .

He forced his mind away from the dread truth of Doban's death, fighting the emptiness with thoughts of other things. Duties. Pleasures. Anger. The fist pounding on the ledge began to bleed, and the blood ran into the pool of water by his feet. Duty . . . Pleasure . . . Anger . . .

The punishment of Shil remained. Shil the meat stealer. Tried according to tradition and found guilty. Only the punishment remained. There were other clans where Shil would be stabbed with knives and the chief would crack the eggshell of his skull and eat his brains. It was a custom Thag thought he might introduce. *Starting with Shil!*

Thag squatted in that private, howling wilderness of loneliness, blindly staring out, immobile save for one great bloody fist that pounded and pounded and pounded and pounded.

A tear squeezed from the corner of his eye and splashed unheeded on the ledge.

5

Tale of Ogres

"An ogre clan?" an elder whispered. "You say you saw an *ogre clan*?"

In the stifling gloom of the longhouse, Hiram felt a trickle of sweat roll down the muscles of his chest. He was aware of the women's eyes, glinting liquid in the firelight, the eyes of the tribal chieftain Renka, the glittering, jet-black eyes of the Crone, the eyes of the elders watching him intently. He sat very upright, aware his heart was pounding, and told his story. He strove to be simple so that they might believe him, although he did not think they would.

"I left our village camp before dawn," he said. He hoped they would not interrupt him. He might be able to get through the whole story without making a fool of himself if they did not ask him questions.

31

"Before dawn?" Renka frowned.

"Before dawn?" echoed Elder Yste.

"Before dawn?" murmured Elder Looca, oldest of them save the Crone. She had a melodious voice, deep almost like that of a man. "Why did you venture from the safety of the camp before dawn?"

Questions. How could he avoid such questions? What sort of fool left the village camp in darkness when the world was full of spirits and hunting beasts? Of course they would ask him questions. But how to answer?

Hiram remembered. But not the adventure in the night, not the horror of the ogres in the half-light. He remembered Shiva once taking his hand in the growing light, pointing to the east and showing him the sunrise. It was not the first dawn he had seen, of course, but it was the first dawn he had *really* seen. And he had seen it properly because he had not looked east at all, but, in surprise, at Shiva's face.

That morning, when Hiram was not yet a man, he had felt the hand take his and seen her point and looked, in surprise, at her face. And there saw something strange—a longing and a wonder.

Hiram looked where she looked and saw the sunrise through her eyes. He felt the life of the day and marveled.

He turned toward her, but she was gone. He had not even noticed when she dropped his hand. But she left something with him—the wonder of the sunrise. Never again was he to see it in any other way. Never again *could* he see it in any other way. He found too there was a change in how he looked at other things.

How could he speak of this? How could he tell the Elder Looca he had risen before dawn, stolen from the camp, foolishly ignored the hunting night beasts, more foolishly risked the displeasure of the spirits, *only to watch the rising sun*? She would think him insane. Worse, she might think him *unmanly*.

He lowered his head and muttered his answer.

"Speak up, Hiram," Renka told him tiredly.

"I don't know, Elder Looca," Hiram said again.

He heard the murmur of amusement and waited for the reprimand, but none came. He looked up and chilled to find the glittering eyes of the Crone upon him, boring deep into his soul. But Renka merely shrugged and said, "No matter. Let the boy have his secrets. Go on."

He took a deep breath and told them.

He was not with a girl, whatever they might think. He was not going to see a girl either, as some of the young men did at night, searching for forbidden caves. He was not even leaving the village camp in total darkness, for the false dawn was upon the world, a dim, gray light that stole across the land.

There was a place beyond the turning of the river—not far from camp, not dangerous . . . not *too* dangerous—where he might climb upon a flat-topped rock to watch the sun appear in the cleft between two mountains. He did not tell the elders this, but only that he left the camp in the half-light before dawn and walked with the river at his left hand. But then an odd thing had happened. A portion of the riverbank collapsed as he walked past, frightening him with the sudden noise. He was unharmed, of course, but took it as an omen and so started back.

"Back?" asked Looca. "Back? You went out for a reason you don't know, walked a little way by the river, then came back?"

Hiram nodded glumly, reading the disbelief in her voice.

"An interesting adventure," Renka said, and smiled. She did not believe him either—the smile told him that clearly.

Hiram swallowed, more than ever aware of their eyes. He closed his own eyes to protect himself from their magic and went on with his tale, for there was nothing else to do.

The collapsed portion of the riverbank had forced him to circle outward from his usual trail, skirting a rocky outcrop, which brought him within sight of the forest.

"You went close to the forest?" Looca asked.

Hiram shook his head. Only a fool went close to the forest. He had moved within sight of the forest, no more. The forest itself was still safely distant. It was then he had seen the ogres.

There were many ogre tales told by the winter fires. Some said they were animals, ugly, stronger than a mammoth, swifter than a hunting cat. Some insisted they were spirits, more correctly demons, who feasted on human flesh. All knew they were monsters, living in the gloomy depths of forests, associated with forbidden caves.

Ogres haunted the imagination of the tribe, like ghosts and demons, more feared than the dreaded nightwing.

None in this generation of the tribe claimed contact with an ogre, although there were many grand tales of ogre slaying in the olden times. It was said the ogre clans avoided human contact now, lurking in dark, supernatural places, ever ready to murder humans foolhardy enough to venture near.

Hiram had not ventured near. He was far from any forbidden cave, far from the depths of the forest where the ogres roamed, but he had seen them, three together, close by the forest edge.

For the first time the Crone spoke, her voice brittle and dry as twigs on a summer fire. "How did you know they were ogres, hunter?"

Hiram felt a shiver travel down his spine, partly because the Crone had spoken directly to him, but more from the memory of what he had seen. "They were so ugly, my lady witch," he said with feeling. "They were *monsters*!"

His words were far from adequate. They were the most terrifying things he had ever seen. They were in the shape of men, but monstrous men. Men too broadly muscled. Men with the jaws of wolves, of tigers. They were demons in the shape of men, night shapes hunting in the stark, gray light of recent dawn. . . .

Hiram ran. He ran as if the gibbering ghosts of sorcerers long dead had risen from the ground to take him. He ran and found a disused den dug out by some forgotten beast and squeezed inside and hid there, trembling.

For a long time he remained, knowing the ogres must find him, must eat his flesh and gnaw his bones. But the ogres did not come, and eventually his heart stilled from its pounding and he emerged like a timid rabbit and cleaned himself using grass still damp from morning dew. He knew he must warn the tribe. No human child was safe while ogres lived—this everyone knew. They were dark magic, and if there were any near, they must be hunted down and killed.

Hiram loved his tribe. There was none like it anywhere on earth. Although he knew how foolish he had looked, how cowardly his actions, he knew he had to warn his tribe. Only later did it occur to him they might not believe him.

He had told his tale. Would they believe him? After the business of the marula grove, would they believe him?

A slow voice he did not recognize at once—the voice of an elder hidden in the shadows of the inner chamber—asked, "Did not the Lightning Bird appear this time, Hiram?"

His spirit turned to stone then. He glanced from face to face, his fear of them crushing his terror for the safety of the tribe.

He read the disbelief on every face.

6
Captured

Sometimes Shiva made pictures in her head, although she told no one about them anymore. She knew that few of the tribe could do this easily, except for the Crone, of course. It was well known the Crone could make pictures of the past and future.

But Shiva's pictures were not of the past or future. She made pictures of a woman she had never known, a woman whose face was difficult to see. And this woman would hold her, rock her, croon the little baby sleep-songs to her. Shiva called this picture-woman Mother, although she was not the Mother Goddess. She would whisper the word aloud, crouched in dark corners, so that she might listen to the sound.

Less often, Shiva would make mind pictures of

a handsome man. His features were clearer than those of the woman: He looked a little like the hunter Hiram, but much older. He was very skilled and very strong. Sometimes in her mind Shiva would picture herself attacked by some great beast—a cave lion, perhaps—and this man would kill the cat to protect her. Then, like the woman in her mind, he would hold her, cradle her and rock her, calling her his daughter.

Shiva found these pictures made her sad, although she did not know why and did not cease to make them in her mind. But she made other pictures too. She saw herself returning from a hunt (which she had led, despite her age and inexperience) carrying the carcass of the kill—reindeer, elk or even a great aurochs bull. In her mind pictures she would return to the village encampment proudly, openly, followed by her hunters, Hiram among them and near her, and the children and the women and the men and the entire Council of the Elder Women would turn out to greet her and to cheer.

She thought of those mind pictures now, because she was returning with a kill. The strange boy was carrying it across his broad shoulders, having ignored her orders to leave it where it lay. It was not an aurochs bull, but there was pride to be taken in a wolf. Any hunter would take pride in a wolf, although she had known of none who could kill one by biting on it with his teeth. She would tell the tribe how the wolf had hunted her and how it had cornered her and how she had attacked it and how it had almost killed her before this boy landed on its back. She glanced back at him plodding doggedly a few paces behind her. She wished he were not so ugly, not so hairy, but it was a good story nonetheless.

All the same, she did not walk in triumph to the village. Habit or caution or some deep-rooted instinct carried her feet in the familiar circle so that she entered the village as she always did, from the side, unnoticed. There were, in any case, few people about. The hunt was out and she suspected there might be a meeting in the longhouse. Shiva stayed well away from the longhouse. She had no business there and hoped she never would. She pointed and the ugly boy seemed to understand, for he dropped the carcass on the ground. Shiva added the skin that she had carried, for it was *his* skin, his kill. Then she waited.

He did nothing, but remained immobile in that curious stooped stance of his, staring at her with liquid eyes.

Shiva gestured. "You must prepare it," she told him impatiently. "Prepare it."

He said nothing. Briefly she wondered if he might be dumb. He had said nothing, uttered no sound, neither when he killed the wolf nor on the walk back. "Prepare it!" she said again. Then, unconsciously echoing the words and tones of some half-forgotten lesson, she added sharply, "Otherwise the meat will spoil and the skin will rot." She handed him her own flint knife.

The boy took the knife and stared at it. He turned it over and over in his hands, tested the edge with his thumb and cut himself quite deeply. Still he made no sound, but stared at the blood welling up with an expression of such comic incredulity that Shiva gave one of her rare smiles. Then he threw the knife angrily to one side and squatted, his thumb plugged into his mouth like that of a baby.

"Don't you know how?" Shiva asked. She mimed gutting the wolf, scraping the pelt. The dark eyes staring out beneath the heavy brows never left her, but he made no move. "You don't know how?" Still no movement. "Can't you talk, boy?" Nothing.

Shiva sighed. "I'll show you," she said. She picked up the knife and stood over the body of the wolf. "It's your kill, but I'll show you—all right?" His eyes never faltered, but he did not seem to mind that she would touch his kill, as he had not seemed to mind when she skinned it. Where had he come

41

from, this strange boy? He acted like no boy she knew, not of her tribe nor any other. No matter. He had saved her from the wolf, and she would show him how to prepare the kill.

She began with the pelt, because it was so much easier. She smoothed it fur side down on the ground and squatted, one foot on it to hold it, left hand stretching it as she used the edge of the knife to scrape away the fat and flesh. "You must take care not to cut the skin," she told him, "but scrape off all the flesh so it dries clean and doesn't smell." She scraped and scraped expertly, for she had done this job many times before with prey from the hunt. "If you can find an anthill, the ants will help you clean it, but you must watch they do not start to eat the pelt itself. If they do, you must brush them off." She grinned. "And then they bite you." Scrape . . . scrape . . . scrape . . .

She chatted to him as she worked, about ants and preparing hides and finding food and the strange way he had killed the wolf. She found him easy to talk to, because he did not move and did not answer back, although his eyes never left her. Only once did he change his position, when he removed his thumb from his mouth to examine the cut. It no longer bled, but he put his thumb back anyway.

42

"You want to keep the fur—yes?" Shiva asked him. "It's warmer to wear if you keep the fur. Of course, if you want to make shoes—*shoes*—" She pointed to her own rough-sandaled feet. "If you want to make leather, you have to take the fur off. But I think you might want to wear this. . . ."

She stood up and examined the skin. She had done a good job: all the flesh removed and no cut in the pelt, not even a small scratch. "Now," she said, signaling again, "you come."

He made no move, but she walked off anyway, since she was going no farther than the remains of one of last night's ringfires, which kept spirits at bay and frightened away the hunting night beasts. When she reached it, he was by her shoulder. She reached down and took a handful of the warm wood ash, which she began to rub into the skin. "This helps draw out the water," she told him carefully. "You must draw out the water, otherwise the hide will rot. Get me some dry wood, will you?" She thought she might coax the fire into life again to smoke the pelt. He remained at her shoulder, staring at the ashy wolfskin. "All right," she said, "all right—*I'll* get the firewood." She sighed again, loudly, so he would hear. Then she remembered she had not brought back the firewood she had gathered and sighed again, more realistically this time. "We'll smoke it later," she said. She looked at him. His eyes never left hers and she shrugged. It was difficult to judge how much he understood, but she suspected it might be very little.

She left the pelt near the dead fire, where the small residue of heat would keep it dry, and went back to the carcass of the wolf. "We have to clean this," she told him. She smiled at him. "Clean it so it will not spoil—you understand?" He did not understand. He could not speak, he could not prepare a pelt. Obviously he did not understand. All the same, she had already talked more to him than she had talked to any boy of the tribe, ever. She found herself . . . liking him. He obviously liked her, the way he followed her around. And as well as liking her, he had saved her from the wolf.

"Clean it," she said again, pointing. He looked at the body of the wolf, then back at her.

She would have preferred the carcass hung from a tree branch, but it was a little heavy for her to manage comfortably and she did not think she could make him understand what would be needed. She grinned to herself as she thought of his blank look if she tried to teach him knots. So the carcass on the ground would have to do. She pinched the abdomen as high as possible and inserted the knife in the pouch of flesh to make an opening wide enough to take two fingers.

"What you got there, Shiva?"

She glanced up to find they had been joined by a group of the little children, wide-eyed and dirty. She liked the little ones better than the children of her own age and sometimes even played with them.

"Wolf," she told them proudly.

"Shiva killed a wolf!" said one to her companions.

"Wow!" said a very little one. "When I'm a hunter, I'm going to kill a woof!"

"Not me," Shiva said. "He—" She looked around, but the ugly boy was nowhere to be seen. "Him . . ." she concluded, wondering. She shrugged and continued gutting the beast.

The children watched her make the upward and the downward cut, then ran off chanting *"Shiva killed a wolf! Shiva killed a wolf! Shiva Shiva killed a killed a Shiva killed a wooooooooolf!"* They ended in a long-drawn-out wolf howl.

The gut began to spill, not as neatly as if the carcass had been hung. She cut to the breastbone, then plunged her hand inside and gently eased out the remainder of the innards. The pungent smell of blood covered all scents, but she felt eyes upon her, and when she glanced around, she discovered the boy had returned and was squatting again, watching her. To her surprise, she felt glad. He was shy, she told herself. She could understand that. He was ugly, hairy, and did not want to be near other people because he was *different*. She could understand that too.

Neatly, she removed the kidneys and the liver. She plunged her hand in and pulled out the gall-bladder in the center, taking care not to burst it and thus taint the meat. She threw the bladder away into the bushes and quickly inspected the liver for white spots. There were none. The wolf had been healthy. She handed it to him. "You eat," she urged. "Good food." It was, but it would not keep. The liver was the seat of the animal's soul and rotted quickly when the soul left. By eating it, the ugly boy would partake of the wolf's courage; as was his right, since he had killed the wolf.

For a moment she thought he might refuse, but he took it and ate it quickly, with rapid movements of his powerful jaw.

"Good?" Shiva asked. "Was that good?" She found herself speaking to him as she might speak to one of the babies who toddled and crawled under the grandmothers' care. She returned to the internal organs, cutting through the chest membrane so she could remove the lungs and heart. "These are the lites," she told him, holding up the lungs. "They are not so good to eat, but you can give them to Hiram for fish bait. And this is the

46

heart—it makes good stew." She began the tedious job of drawing out the intestines, which Elder Looca sometimes liked to stuff with meat and herbs and roast over a slow fire. "What we do with—"

"*Ogre!*" a voice screamed, "*Ogre!*"

Shiva looked up in alarm. The ugly boy had jumped to his feet and was spinning around, a faint growl rumbling in the back of his throat. They were surrounded by a group of hunters, led by Leena, who was skilled in trapping and ambushing game. The sight of them frightened the boy, who darted back and forth in panic but could not escape.

"*Ogre!*" screamed the voice again. It was Mano, one of the oldest hunters.

"Catch him," Leena ordered crisply.

Shiva saw immediately what was happening. Ogre? Why did they call him ogre? But the word had burned its way into her mind and suddenly she saw him differently. All the stories flooded back, the tales of ogres eating human flesh. In that instant she believed none of them. But *could* he be a young ogre?

The growling in his throat became a howl as the hunters hurled themselves upon him. He fought, gouging with his fingers, snapping with his teeth. But he went down beneath a writhing heap of bodies.

Shiva's paralysis broke. "No!" she screamed,

throwing herself on the nearest hunter's back, trying to pull him away. "No, don't hurt him! Please don't hurt him! He saved me from the wolf!"

She kicked and scratched and fought, screaming and pleading. But they held her easily enough and took the little ogre away.

7

Hiram Chosen

A small, drab bird strutted to the utmost edge of an overhanging bough and stared down curiously at Hiram, head tilted, the better to regard him with one glittering black, beady eye.

"Shoo!" Hiram muttered. But he was too disconsolate to move, so the bird remained impertinently where it was. He stared back at it unseeing, through a pervasive fog of fear. His worries rolled across him in successive billows . . . the danger to the tribe . . . this latest humiliation . . . the punishment the elders might inflict on him.

As he waited to hear the elders' reaction to his news of the ogres, he worried fearfully about all these things. But most of all, he worried about the Sacred Drums.

Hiram still remembered the first time he had seen the Sacred Drums. He had been little more than a baby then, a lively creature, able to crawl much farther than most children of his age and so intensely curious that he was always getting into trouble. In a frenzy of impatience he had disturbed the careful arrangement of skulls and bones on the floor of the cave where the Sacred Drums were kept. It occurred to Hiram that he was still getting into trouble even now. The elders had said nothing to his face, but he knew, beyond doubt, they believed he was lying. It was understandable, of course.

The elders were meeting now in the gloom of the longhouse, deciding what to do about the liar Hiram. Looca and Yste and the dreadful Crone were all muttering their contributions to his fate. He did not think he actually faced death or banishment, but there were possibilities that, in their own ways, were worse.

Hiram knew that if the elders did not believe him, the tribe risked great danger. To face ogres unprepared was to invite disaster. And if they did not believe him, they would certainly be unprepared.

Unless, of course, the ogres decided not to attack. There were ancient tales of times when humans had met ogres and avoided war, but only when some great magic was involved. If the elders did not believe he had seen the ogres, they would prepare no magic. The Sacred Drums would not be beaten.

Hiram thought back to the second time he saw the drums, when he was older and could understand more. . . .

There were five in all, each carved from a single block of wood. The largest was some two feet in diameter, with cross-strut handles and a drumhead made from antelope skin stretched and pegged onto a series of holes burned around the rim. The smallest, which showed only a cylindrical knob as a handle, was decorated in a raised tooth pattern. All were smooth, dark, shiny and worn from many generations' use.

Hiram stood rigid, almost at attention, caught up in the aura of respect his mother showed toward the drums. She called them koma, *sometimes* dikomana, *and he knew now they were sacred drums.*

As they stood before the drums, his mother whispered a dark secret in the form of an old proverb: "The man who makes the dikomana will see them with his eyes, but he will never hear them with his ears."

Without speaking further, she moved to the largest drum ("the big cow" as she called it) and reverently removed some pegs and rolled back a portion of the stretched drumhead. She beckoned Hiram, and he moved reluctantly to stare into the body of the drum.

51

The big cow, the largest drum of all, which could only be beaten by hand, contained the skull of the man who made it.

Human sacrifice, his mother said, was no longer carried out. But it had been the custom of the dreamtime and gave great power, great magic, to the dikomana.

The drums were used for the greatest of all tribal magics—for protection of the hunt, for protection of the tribe, for initiation of a Crone. Without the Sacred Drums, the tribe would quickly wither away and die. Such was the magic of the drums. They were gods.

The Keeper of the Sacred Drums was someone of great importance to the tribe. The office was hereditary, passed generation by generation from parent to child in an ancient line. Sheena, Hiram's mother, was the Keeper of the Sacred Drums.

As they stood before the Sacred Drums, Sheena told Hiram the terrifying news that he, Hiram, might at some stage in the future himself become the Keeper of the Sacred Drums.

The realization thrilled, then frightened him.

And now, as he waited for the decision of the elder council, the news haunted him. For if they thought him untruthful, it would surely mean he could never become the Keeper of the Sacred Drums.

"Hiram?"

Hiram looked up to see the dark, pretty girl bending over him. He looked at her unspeaking, so frightened he was scarcely able to breathe. Distantly, at the far end of the village camp, he was aware of some confusion and excitement, but was too much a prey to his personal concerns to think what might be the cause.

"Renka wishes you to see her," the young woman said, unsmiling.

"The elders—?" Hiram began to ask.

But she cut him short. "Renka wishes you to see her now."

So his fate was sealed. He stood up and followed the girl back to the longhouse, where she left him at the entrance to the inner chamber. He hesitated through a long eternity, then went in because there was nowhere else to go.

The chamber was empty except for the solitary figure of Renka, the tribal chief. Renka would deliver the judgment. Renka would tell him he was disbelieved. Renka would inform him he was no longer worthy to become the Keeper of the Sacred Drums.

Her face was set, stern and impatient. She glanced at him as he entered, almost as if surprised to see him.

"Elder Renka—" he began, not knowing what

it was he meant to say. She silenced him with a gesture.

"Hiram," she said, "the news you bring is grave and requires action."

Action. There might perhaps be punishment, however undeserved.

"Many of my sisters consider you too young for what must be done—"

Too young? His age might be taken as an excuse!

"But the Crone has seen and thus it must be."

"Elder Renka—" Hiram said again, desperation creeping into his voice.

"Courage!" Renka said. "The decision is made. The Crone has seen, the elders have spoken. It is you, Hiram, who must lead those who will rid us of the threatened evil."

"Lead?" echoed Hiram.

"Lead our tribe's warriors against the ogres."

"Against . . . ?"

"The ogres," repeated Renka.

Before he could quite stop himself, Hiram blurted, "You believed me?"

Renka blinked, bewildered. "Of course we believed you! Why should we not believe you?" She looked away from him, her face like stone. "Besides, we have already captured one of the accursed brood."

8

Taken by the Strangers

They huddled together in the deep caves, Thag's huge arms around her, sharing body heat. Hana's hands unpicked the tangles in his hair, nervously grooming, fearfully searching.

"He is dead, Thag."

"He is dead, Hana." The pictures flooded through his mind like torrents of meltwater. He imagined Doban mauled by the cave lion, bitten by the snake, swept away by the flood, trapped in the crevice, buried by the landslide, fallen from the tree. He could not choose between these several nightmares, but it did not matter. Neither Thonar, Kral, Mabango, nor Dan had managed to pick up his track. Not even Heft the Hunter, the finest tracker in the clan, could find him. The boy had disappeared and thus was dead. A part of Thag had died with him.

"You searched far, Thag," Hana said.

As they had, by the ancestors and all the gods! They had searched the caverns and the deep forest, hunted in the rocklands and the riverside, but it was as if Doban had never been. When they returned, Hagar whispered that perhaps they should inquire of all who might have seen the boy, and he, Thag, chief of all the clan, had done so, growling and with threatening gestures so that none should dare to lie. But no one had seen him. It was as he expected, for Doban was a brave boy—too brave, perhaps.

Thag remembered, watching the pictures unfold before his mental eye. He, Thag, mightiest of all the clan, was showing his son Doban how to hunt small game in the deep forest. Small game to suit Doban, who himself was small then, for these were pictures from a time eight seasons distant. Thag watched the hare in the clearing, watched Doban hurl himself upon it, watched the wildcat that sought to rob him of his prey.

Thag had blundered from the forest, roaring like an enraged bull, intent on saving the boy. But by the time he reached them, the wildcat was already dead, heart pierced by Doban's little blade. Doban's face and body were raked savagely by wildcat claws, his arm deeply bitten, his blood streaming everywhere. Proud wounds, and Thag took him proudly home, where Hana shrieked abuse at him for permitting the boy to come to harm. Thag smiled at the memory. Women knew nothing of these things, nothing. Hana had seen only the blood and the pain and not the pride with which the boy bore his wounds.

"Why are you smiling, Thag?"

How could she tell in the dark? How was it she could always tell? "I was remembering," Thag growled and felt her nod.

"He was a good boy," Hana said.

"He was a brave boy," Thag corrected her. "Brave and strong." He shifted slightly to ease a growing cramp. "Like his father," he added.

"Like his father," Hana echoed. "You searched well."

Such a search, thought Thag. Such a search there had never been in the whole history of the clan. He had searched well, as she said. But not well enough.

After a long moment, he placed his mouth by Hana's ear and whispered like Hagar, "What of his soul?"

"His soul?" Hana asked.

"His soul, woman!" Thag whispered urgently. Women knew of such things.

57

"His soul will fly," said Hana mildly. "It will fly like a bird and seek another body to be born."

"He will be . . . happy?"

"Oh yes, he will be happy."

Thag shifted again, uneasily. The mysteries of birth, death and rebirth were women's work, and he felt uncomfortable among them. When a member of the clan died, the women took the body and bound it, knees to chest, arms curled, ready to be born again. Then they took the earth's blood, red ocher, and anointed it, for blood was life. Finally they placed it in a cave or fissure, covered with flowers and facing east toward the rising sun so the dead eyes might see the light of another day.

"You have not tied his body or anointed it with earth's blood," Thag whispered.

"How could I tie his body or anoint it when you have not found his body?" Hana snapped. He felt her stiffen. "Mindless clod!"

"Will his soul still be reborn?" Thag hissed. "Will it, Hana? Without the earth's blood, will his soul still be reborn?"

He felt her little hands flutter over him, gently as a butterfly. "Yes," she said softly, "his soul will be reborn."

They remained thus, holding one another, for a long time, each lost in the corridors of memory, each drawing strength from the other, communing silently through touch, small movement and proximity. The darkness pressed upon them.

Thag began to weep then, in the darkness, where none of the clan could see him, his massive body racked with sobs. Hana slid her arms around his neck and cradled his head to her breast and held him as she might hold a child. She said nothing, for there was no relief in words, but only rocked him gently and waited. Eventually the weeping stopped.

"Will you punish Shil?" Hana asked.

Thag shrugged. "No."

"He stole Heft's meat."

"It does not matter." He was surprised to hear himself say it did not matter, although he knew it was true. Perhaps Heft had lost his meat. Perhaps Shil had really stolen it. It did not matter. There would always be men who would steal, if not Shil then some other. And if not men, an animal might creep into a cave and take meat. Who could say— and what matter anyway? Nothing seemed important anymore.

"Shil wishes to be chief," he said.

"Shil has always wished to be chief," said Hana softly.

"Would he make a good chief?"

"He is strong," Hana said.

"Not as strong as me."

"No, not as strong as you. No man has your strength."

"I feel I am grown old, Hana."

"Yes, I know."

"Perhaps I should let Shil be chief."

"That would not bring back Doban," Hana said.

"No," Thag said, "it would not." He growled suddenly, far back in his throat. "I shall not let Shil be chief, nor any other."

"Good," Hana said, and she kissed him.

A looming form entered the cave, moving silent as a cat despite its bulk. From the scent, Thag knew it to be Heft the Hunter. He dropped down beside them and embraced Hana and beyond her Thag, so that all three huddled in the darkness. Hana stroked his hair, which was finer than Thag's and less tangled.

"I have found Doban," said Heft the Hunter.

Thag felt Hana suddenly rigid in his arms. "Doban's body?" she asked, abruptly breathless.

"Doban," Heft said. "Doban lives."

His words hung in the darkness, bright and luminous like pictures in the mind.

"You are sure?" asked Hana. "You are sure he lives?"

There came the movement of broad shoulders, shrugging in the darkness. "I am Heft the Hunter," Heft said simply.

They clung together, all three, then Thag broke apart from them and ran around the inner cavern in the darkness. His fists smashed limestone spurs and pounded on the floor. A growling roar came from his throat, reverberating out through the galleries. When his circuit was complete, he squatted to embrace them warmly.

"We looked everywhere," said Thag.

"Everywhere," Heft echoed.

"I ordered the search finished," said Thag, "and I am chief."

"Hush, Thag," Hana said. "Let Heft tell it." He could feel her trembling with excitement. "Tell it quickly, Heft, for I must see him."

"You are chief," said Heft, ignoring her, "but Doban is your son."

"Forgive his disobedience, idiot!" Hana hissed impatiently.

"I forgive your disobedience," Thag muttered. He would have to speak severely to her. Sometimes she completely failed to recognize his dignity as chief. He would have to speak *most* severely to her. But not just now. Not now when Heft had found Doban! He almost smiled, but caught himself in time and turned to frown severely in the direction of Heft's scent.

"I tracked beyond the forest," Heft said. "I have skill in tracking."

"You are the greatest tracker in the clan," Thag acknowledged. Heft's reputation as a tracker extended throughout every cavern of every clan.

"There was no track in the forest, but beyond the forest, I picked up Doban's trail. Why should he leave the forest? I cannot say, but who can say what a boy may do? I followed the trail. At times I thought I had lost it, yet still I followed it."

"None could have followed it but Heft," Thag said.

"Quickly, Heft—quickly!"

"It led me to the camp of the Weakling Strangers," Heft said bluntly.

Thag heard her gasp, felt the stiffness return to her body. He too felt fear, his innards turned to water. The Weakling Strangers . . . was there ever such a name?

They had come in the time of his father's father— or before. Who could remember such things? Enough that they had come. They came from the south, hairless, ugly, puny things that mocked the shape of men. They were light-colored, like the spirits of the dead, malformed in their heads, lacking the handsome brow-ridge that protected from the sun, with noses like the beaks of birds, weak jaws, unable to crack a thighbone, weak shoulders, weak arms, weak legs, weak bodies. The Weakling Strangers they were called by all who saw them.

But the Weakling Strangers killed the greatest and the strongest of the clans, hunted and trapped them, slew them in their tens and in their hundreds. The Weakling Strangers stalked the game trails, murdering any true man who came near. Their women ruled them and made magic of such strength no creature of the clans could stand against it. They took the best sites for their camps, the best-stocked hunting grounds for game. And everywhere they killed the people of the clans.

War came then, the first war any in the clans remembered. But what could the people do? The Weakling Strangers would not let them live in peace. They stole the land, they stole the game, they killed and killed and killed. Thus clan warriors fought back. And while the weakest among them was stronger by far than the strongest Stranger, yet the Strangers won. The magic of the women won. None in the clans could stand against it. This was in Thag's father's father's time, or before. It was called the Age of Blood, the blood of the true people, the blood of the clans.

Oh, they were brave men. They fought as men had never fought before.

But no man could stand against the women's magic, and the clans grew dangerously weak. Their best hunters had turned warrior. The Strangers took the easy game and few among the clans were left to hunt the rest. Hunger came to the clans. In Thag's father's father's time, for the first time in their history, the clans knew unremitting hunger, stretching day by day, moon after moon. With hunger there was sickness, sickness such as the true people had never known. The wise ones said the gods and ancestors were angry, the clans had sinned in some way and were punished for it. But none could tell the nature of the sin, or the means of atonement. And still the people died.

At last, in Thag's father's father's time, or before, the chiefs decreed the war must cease. There was an old man then, by name Drak, not himself a chief or a hunter, but an advisor like Hagar, heavy with years, white-haired and full of wisdom, with the ear of a great chief. Drak advised that the clans must henceforth hide from these terrible invaders, must hide in the forests and the deep caves, must hide in the night, must avoid the Weakling Strangers at all costs.

So it was. Not all the clans agreed, but those who

did not were hunted by the Weakling Strangers and died out. The rest, as Drak advised, melted into the forests and deep caves, discovered new ways to hunt or gathered food from the forest floor, and hid so successfully from the Strangers that the Strangers ceased to think of them, began to look upon them as they looked on spirits—something distant, something not quite . . . real. So it remained. The Strangers moved from place to place as was their custom. At their approach, the people of the clans hid themselves away, remaining hidden until the Strangers had passed on. Only thus was there safety for the people of the clans.

But no safety for Doban now.

"Before I reached the camp of the Strangers, I scented wolf," Heft was saying.

"He was taken by a wolf!" gasped Hana. She clutched Thag fiercely.

"He was not taken by a wolf," said Heft, "for wolves fear people and—"

"A wolf will sometimes attack!" hissed Hana. "Sometimes!"

"Quiet, woman," Thag growled without conviction. He too feared Doban might have been taken by a wolf.

"He was not taken," Heft said calmly, "for the wolf is dead and Doban is alive. He was not taken by the wolf, but he has been taken by the Strangers."

It was said.

The words echoed in the caverns of Thag's mind. *Taken . . . Taken by the Strangers . . . Taken . . .* He broke away from Hana and from Heft and began to lope round the darkened cave, one hand on the wall for guidance, growling deep in his throat.

"He is alive?" he heard Hana ask.

"The Strangers have him, but he is alive."

"We must get him back," said Hana firmly, without hesitation.

Thag threw back his huge head and roared into the darkness. "I will kill the Weakling Strangers! I will slaughter them! I will tear them to pieces as the great cats tear apart a deer! I am the chief! I am the strongest of the clan! I will bring back my son!"

There was a great silence in the cavern then, with scarcely the sound of breathing. Eventually Hana's voice said, "You will not go alone."

9

Legend of Saber

Nothing—nothing of importance—ever happens by accident.

Three years before, when she was aged no more than a hundred moons, Shiva found the Ring of Stones. . . .

She knew at once where she was. The central megalith, towering skyward at an angle, was of gray-black granite flecked with mica and quite unmistakable. It was larger by far than she had ever imagined, so thick at the base that a herd of aurochs might have hidden behind it, and soaring upward like a cliff face. The boulders lying around its base were so huge, she wondered how the ancient tribes had moved them there. Yet move them they had, for Shiva knew the ancient story of Saber well. . . .

Long ago, in the dreamtime, there lived a wildcat named Saber who wished to be chief among all creatures. "And why should it not be so?" he asked himself. "For am I not the largest wildcat in the world?" As indeed he was, for Saber was clever and skilled and fed well.

But one day while drinking at the waterhole, the wildcat Saber met a cat who was larger than he, a creature with a stubby tail and tufted ears. "How can this be?" asked Saber. "I am the largest wildcat in the world, yet you are larger."

"That is because I am not a wildcat," said the creature with the tufted ears. "I am a short-tailed lynx and thus bigger than any wildcat."

So Saber went to the Mother of All Things and said to her, "Mother, how may I, a wildcat, grow larger than the short-tailed lynx and thus become chief among creatures?"

The Mother was amused at this pretty speech and decided to play a trick on Saber. "I shall tell you where to find the Pool of Growth," she said. "Go there and swim in the water, and you will grow large as any short-tailed lynx. But take care you do not drink the water, otherwise you will surely regret it. And you must never visit the Pool of Growth without my permission." And she smiled to herself, knowing how cats hate water and thinking that Saber would not do it.

68

But Saber followed the directions of the Mother and found the Pool of Growth and, biting back his loathing of water, swam in it and grew at once larger than any short-tailed lynx.

For a time he was content.

Then one day at the waterhole, Saber met another cat who was larger than he, a creature with a long tail and spots upon its coat. "How can this be?" asked Saber. "I am the largest wildcat or short-tailed lynx in the world, yet you are larger."

"That is because I am neither a wildcat nor a short-tailed lynx," said the creature. "I am a spotted leopard and thus larger than either."

So Saber went back to the Mother of All Things and said to her, "Mother, how may I, a wildcat, grow larger than the spotted leopard and thus become chief among creatures?"

"Return to the Pool of Growth," the Mother said, "and swim twice in the water, and you shall grow larger than any leopard. But take care not to swallow a single drop of the water, otherwise you will surely regret it. And be certain you do not visit the Pool of Growth without my permission."

So Saber returned to the Pool of Growth and, biting back his loathing, swam twice in it and grew larger than any spotted leopard.

And for a time he was content.

Then one day at the waterhole, he met a tawny

cat who was much larger than he. "How can this be?" asked Saber. "I am the largest wildcat or short-tailed lynx or spotted leopard in the world, yet you are larger."

"That is because I am neither a wildcat nor a short-tailed lynx nor a spotted leopard," said the creature. "I am a maned cave lion and thus larger than all three. What is more, I am favored by the Mother of All Things, who has promised that no cat shall ever grow larger than me."

At this, the wildcat Saber became very thoughtful, for he knew that if he returned to the Mother of All Things and asked her permission to swim in the Pool of Growth she would not give it, on account of her promise to the cave lion.

"No matter," said Saber to himself. "For I know where the Pool of Growth is hidden, and I will bathe in the water without the Mother's knowledge and thus grow larger than the maned cave lion." And so he did.

Thus it was that Saber became larger than any other wildcat, larger than a short-tailed lynx, larger than a spotted leopard, larger even than the maned cave lion who was so large that he could bring down an aurochs cow. And Saber strutted the plains of the dreamtime, believing himself now to be the chief among all creatures.

But one day at the waterhole he met a creature so large that he, Saber, seemed no bigger than a shrew-mouse by comparison. It had legs like tree trunks, small, half-hidden ears, a coat as proudly shaggy as a cave lion's mane and great curling tusks that soared toward the clouds.

"How can this be?" asked Saber. "I am the largest wildcat or short-tailed lynx or spotted leopard or maned cave lion in the world, yet you are larger."

"That is because I am not a cat at all," said the creature. "I am a woolly mammoth and thus larger than all cats or any other creature."

This worried Saber greatly, for he had never before seen any living thing so big and powerful, and he knew that even if he were to swim in the Pool of Growth from morning until night, he would never grow as large as the woolly mammoth. Thus he returned to the Mother of All Things and said, "Mother, how may I grow so that I become bigger than the woolly mammoth, for while I remain smaller than him, how shall I be chief among all creatures?"

But the Mother saw that Saber had already grown larger than was natural for a cat, larger not only than a lynx or a leopard but larger even than a cave lion, who she had promised would be the

71

largest of all cats. And she knew he must have returned to the Pool of Growth without her permission.

So she said to him, "Saber, you have already grown too large for your own good. You must be content with what you are and seek no more to grow larger than the woolly mammoth, whom I have decreed to be the largest of all living creatures. No more must you visit the Pool of Growth, and especially must you avoid drinking thereof, otherwise my anger will be visited upon you."

"I hear you, Mother of All Things," Saber said, "and I will obey." But in his heart he knew he would not obey, for he wished above all else to become chief among creatures. Thus, at dead of night he crept to the Pool of Growth and instead of swimming, drank the water, for he believed the Mother had forbidden it to him only because it would allow him to grow as large as he wished and become the largest of all living creatures.

At once, Saber was plunged into a deep sleep. And when he awoke, he was no larger than he had been before, but his two front teeth had grown so enormous that they seemed like mammoth's tusks. But while the mammoth's tusks curled upward, Saber's teeth curved down. He stared at his reflection in the waters of the pool and saw he was no longer the handsome cat he had once been, but a monster in feline form.

But instead of blaming his plight on his own ambition and disobedience, as was the truth of it, Saber instead blamed the Mother of All Things and vowed to himself that he should have his vengeance upon her.

Thus he hid in a tree and when the Mother walked below him, dropped upon her as the leopard drops upon his prey. But the Mother caught hold of one of his huge curved teeth and threw him from her back.

"Why do you attack me, cat?" the Mother asked then. "Do you not know I am the Mother of All Things and thus the mother of you?"

"I know this," growled Saber. "I attack you because you would not allow me to grow larger than the mammoth and thus become chief of all creatures."

When the Mother heard this, she became very angry and picked up a great finger of stone, larger than any other stone in the dreamtime, and threw it at Saber. But Saber was skilled as well as large and jumped aside so that the stone did not strike him. Yet he was very frightened by its size, for it was larger by far than any stone even a mammoth could have moved, and he realized the Mother of

All Things was and ever would be the most powerful of all things.

Thus he ran from her and ran from the dreamtime and hid himself away in dark places and was seldom seen thereafter—and never when the Mother walked abroad.

The great stone, a pillar of granite higher than a tree, was thrown with such force that it too passed out of the dreamtime and fell to earth.

There it embedded itself upright in the ground like a thrown spear and remained forever. When women and men came to walk the surface of the earth, they knew the place to be a holy place because the stone had been touched by the Mother. In olden times a council of the wisest elders ordained that a ring of boulders should be placed around it; and this was done by many men straining under the direction of a Crone.

So there came into being that place that was known to all the tribes as the Ring of Stones, the most secret and holy of all secret places, known only to the Crone of each tribe, barred forever to men and spoken of in whispers even by the women.

Shiva felt a chill of fear as she stood within the great ring.

The ground between the boulders and the central stone was rough and dry and almost barren, but here and there, she could see clumps of smallish, vaguely treelike plants with white, funnel-shaped flowers and hanging, thorny fruit. At the center, where the great stone pierced the earth, they grew more abundantly, forming a wavering white carpet.

Shiva's breath locked in her chest. It was rumored that the spirits of the ancestors gathered in the holy places, as did the spirits of the winds and even, though rarely, gods like Mamar and Hakar and the Kondarabanda. Such creatures were best left alone. All the same, she did not run, for she could scarcely tear her eyes away from that massive granite spear. No wonder Saber had run frightened when the Mother threw it.

She hesitated, half in fear, half in caution. At the northern rim of the slight depression in which the ring lay was a stand of trees that might give cover to a beast. And to the west were rocky outcrops different from the pointing stone, among which anything might lurk. Young as she was, alone as she was, rebellious as she sometimes was, she knew well that those who took no care soon died. Thus she stood for a long time, watching and waiting, her nostrils flaring as she sniffed the air.

75

Her feet moved of their own accord and she walked toward the central stone. Its sheer size was beyond her comprehension, beyond anything she had ever seen.

Dare she touch it, as the Mother had once touched it? To do so would be almost like touching the Mother herself. Shivers began to chase down Shiva's spine.

She pushed through the carpet of white flowers until she was only feet away from the stone; and as her feet had moved, so her hand moved, but she stopped herself when her flat palm was only inches away from the granite surface. Did she dare? Would the Mother be angry?

She looked directly up and the great stone began to sway. Fear welled up from her stomach until she realized it was not the stone but she who swayed. The cloying scent of the white flowers was all around her, like a sweet corruption. She reached out her hand again, as much to steady herself as anything, and actually touched the stone.

"Come away," a dry, harsh voice commanded her.

Shiva whirled around and almost fell. Her mind was suddenly confused and she felt ill in her stomach. How had anyone come so close without her knowing? How had she not heard? How had she not scented? Then she saw and knew. Glittering black eyes locked onto her own and her insides turned to water. "I meant no harm, Lady," she said quickly. "I did not mean to touch the Mother's stone."

The Crone only gazed at her intently. "Come away, child," she said again, impatiently but without anger. "The flowers are making you ill."

"The flower—?"

"The flowers. The white flowers. Have you eaten the seeds or fruit?"

Shiva shook her head, bewildered. "No."

"Then come away!" the Crone snapped. "Come to me—I don't bite!" She blinked slowly, like a reptile, then added, "Whatever they might tell you."

Shiva moved reluctantly toward her and, in so doing, emerged from the dense clump of white flowers. Like everyone else in the tribe, she was frightened of the Crone.

"Thorn apple," said the Crone. "Even the perfume from the flowers is poisonous." The slow blink came again. "Who told you where to find the Ring of Stones, child?"

"No one, Lady. I happened here by accident."

But the Crone, who worked dark magic and could see the future and the past, gave a small,

77

tight smile and whispered, "Nothing—nothing of importance—ever happens by accident."

Shiva thought of the Crone now, as she watched the little ogre, and the witch's words rose up like serpents in her mind. *Nothing—nothing of importance—ever happens by accident.* The men had woven a cage of strong branches lashed with leather thongs and vines. They had put the little ogre into it and hung it with a twisted rope high above the ground from the overhanging branch of a tall tree. It swung and spun in the chill spring winds.

Nothing—nothing of importance—ever happens by accident.

The little ogre crouched, unable to stand upright or lie stretched straight. His head was bowed, his shoulders slumped, his arms hugged tightly across his belly. He neither moved nor called out nor made any sound. Below, the smaller children taunted him and hurled sticks and pebbles at the cage. Some struck home, although with no great force.

Shiva watched him from a hillock just outside the encampment, the newly treated wolfskin pulled across her shoulders to ward off the wind. No one had thought to take it from her. No one was interested in anything other than the little ogre.

Shiva killed a wolf, the little ones chanted in her head. *Shiva Shiva killed a killed a Shiva killed a woooooolf!* But she hadn't. The little ogre had killed the wolf and saved Shiva's life in the process.

Nothing—nothing of importance—ever happens by accident.

What did you do if someone saved your life? What did you do if they took that someone and hung him in a cage? What did you do when all the talk was how he should be executed . . . and how soon?

The cage swung and spun, holding her eyes.

10
The Crone

Shiva moved with care and confidence. This was not the first time she had been out at night, and even though the ringfires were high and the guards more alert than usual, she had little difficulty in avoiding them.

She had no fear of the night, no fear of the darkness. Some of the children—and especially those old enough to know better—insisted evil spirits stalked the night lands. Others claimed the Crone worked magic then. Shiva believed none of it, and never had.

In the dry depths of a cave no other would dare enter, the Crone prepared.

Beyond the cleft, in the cave, were some tools of her mystic trade: pointed goat horns, curling ram horns, the skulls of elk and men, wild cat hide, mammoth tusks, claws strung on animal sinew, knucklebones, reindeer antlers, rhino horn, bat wings, lizard teeth, polished stones, lion fangs . . .

But in the cleft itself, the Crone's aged fingers crumbled dried plants, shredded leaves and stems, shaved aromatic wood chips with a flint blade onto the little heap before her. Wild celery . . . speedwell . . . water lily . . . the tiny five-leafed creeping cinquefoil . . . sweet flag . . . water parsnip . . .

She hummed and rocked as she worked, her hands like spotted squirrels that played and darted in the darkness. She worked by smell and touch alone, occasionally tasting to confirm what her other senses told her. She worked with confidence.

And now the greater magic, requiring plants much more dangerous than those she had used so far. Water hemlock . . . tormentil . . . wolfbane . . . black nightshade . . . henbane . . . mandrake . . . thorn apple . . . poppy . . . Now she no longer tasted, but worked slowly, with infinite care, crumbling, shredding. Before her, resting on a smear of wood ash on the cleft floor, the little heap grew larger.

Finally it was done. She reached for the firestone laid to her left side, the flint to her right, then crooned a soft keening note as she brought them sharply together. Sparks flared, lighting up her lined face like a lightning flash. She struck again and again and at last it caught, a flame that guttered almost instantly, then died.

But it left a pinpoint glow behind. The Crone blew through her lips and the pulsing glow gave her the frightening appearance of an animated corpse, eyes half closed, lips pursed.

Suddenly there was fire. The Crone sat back on her heels and waited. The tinder burned fiercely for a moment and caught a lattice of dry sticks, which flared and crackled like the quiet chatter of old friends. A thick plume of gray-white smoke curled upward, scented with herbs.

The Crone turned and used both hands to lift a yellowing, well-used bowl, created ages past by sawing through a human skull. It was filled almost to overflowing with water stained deep blue by a plant dye. She set it on the ground before her, taking care that none should spill. Somewhere on the outer edges of her mind she sensed the ancestral spirits begin to gather in the cave.

She leaned forward and inhaled the smoke.

The familiar moment wrapped around her. In an instant, all was still, as if the world were waiting. She rocked backward, feeling small pains drain from old limbs, muscle knots relax. A heaviness crept through her body.

She leaned forward again to inhale the smoke. Her lungs burned, but the sensation was no longer unpleasant. She could hear a sound, like the roaring of a distant waterfall, then a faint *click* from within her skull.

The Crone reached down and took the bowl between both hands. In the gloom, points of light danced and tumbled in its depths. It seemed she was falling gently forward, toward the water in the bowl. Her brown eyes closed, and the Crone began to *see*.

The ringfires were lit around the perimeter of the camp, and shadowy figures moved between them, tending them. No beasts would approach while the ringfires burned, and even spirits stayed away unless specifically called. Tonight there were many ringfires because word of the ogres had spread and the tribe was nervous.

In her mind the Crone *saw* Hiram, no longer sleeping in the house of men, but curled solitary and fitful in a small, newly built shelter of his own, as befitted one whose destiny it was to lead the warriors. She could smell the fear scent from him, even in his sleep. The task was thrust upon him, not willingly accepted even now. He was a skilled hunter, lacking only experience to make him one of the finest the tribe had known. And he had courage, like so many who knew fear and sought to overcome it. Yet there was something in him that revolted at the thought of war, even war against the ogre clans.

The Crone's *sight* insinuated itself into the house of women. They slept peacefully enough despite the ogre threat. There too were the children, some with their mothers, some snuggled together in their own separate sleeping tribe. She could hear the gentle snores, the small moans and cries of sleep. All was well here. Except . . . the girl Shiva was not among the children, not among the women.

Wreathed in the white smoke of her herb fire in the chimney niche of her deep cave, the Crone nodded thoughtfully. Shiva was still young. Not *too* young, perhaps, to seek the company of a handsome boy, but she had shown no interest yet in boys, handsome or not. Where, then, had she gone?

Shiva was a strange one, stranger even than Hiram. A solitary child, one who thought much, one who—and here the Crone sighed deeply, so that her entire body shook—had the ogre gift of pictures in the mind and needed special watching because of it. Where would such a child go in the darkness of the night? Those who had the gift were near impossible to predict, even when young.

The Crone's *sight* took her to the shelter of the

chief. Renka was still awake, squatting near the doorway, staring out at a ringfire, lost in thought. There was a fear smell from her too. Renka feared for the tribe.

Renka was a good leader, cautious, thoughtful, slow to anger, yet decisive and ruthless when need be. She was a woman of great practicality. She knew how to select hunters and organize a hunt. She knew how much smoked meat should be stored for the winter. She knew when the tribe should move and when the tribe should stay.

But these were all things she could see and touch and taste and smell, matters of practical experience. When it came to other, more important matters, Renka was a half believer. Renka only half believed that when a woman died, her spirit was embraced by the Mother, only half believed the ancestors still visited the tribe, only half believed in the reality of Mamar, God of Ice, or Hakar, God of Winds, or Kondarabanda, Goddess of All Growing Things.

Worse still, Renka only half believed in ogres.

Now she sat, worried and confused, staring at a ringfire that would form no pictures in her mind. She had almost dismissed Hiram's report, believing him a boy given to exaggeration. She had argued with the elders that he had already proved this with his story of the sacred grove; and because she was chief, she had all but swayed them. Clearly the vote would have gone against him had not chance intervened.

But even now, with the ogre cub captured and caged, Renka did not quite believe in ogres, nor the deadly danger that now crept toward the tribe. Because she did not quite believe, she did not think clearly. She thought of ogres as she thought of bears or wolves or lions—fierce and dangerous and worthy of respect, but animals for all that who were no match for humankind.

Thus she had seen no further than to organize her warriors and prepare them for their task. She called it war, because that was the word the old ones used, but she saw it only as a special kind of hunt. She expected the men to hunt down the three ogres Hiram had seen and bring her back their bodies. But she did not expect danger to the tribe. She could not comprehend a danger so appalling that it threatened the whole tribe.

And yet she was too good a chief not to heed her deepest instincts. It was those instincts, unrecognized, that kept her sleepless now, staring wordlessly into the ringfire, feeling fear she did not understand.

The Crone's *sight* traveled on. She inspected the guards whose duty it was to feed the ringfires and warn of any danger in the night. All seemed far more alert than usual; not one slept. Worry about the ogres kept them moving from one fire to another, muttering reassurances to each other, sniffing the air and peering out into the darkness beyond the thorn fence.

In the cleft of the cave, the Crone stretched to ease the cramps growing in her body. Her watchful tour of the encampment was close to finished; soon she should speak with the gathered spirits. She felt the urge to do so even now, for they were a comfort to her, but some instinct drew her back to the camp, some warning voice insisted there was something she must do, something she should know. The Crone waited.

Where was the girl Shiva?

Shiva moved cautiously now, avoiding the ring-fires, following a familiar route through the camp. Her fear was not of evil spirits or monsters, but of consequences. There was no fear of getting caught, for getting caught no longer mattered. What she planned was so terrible, she could scarcely imagine where the act would lead.

Two guards, both men, had come together and were talking of an exploit in a recent hunt when a wounded boar had turned to gore a hunter. Shiva slid past them like a shadow, moving downwind in an instinctive urge to hide her scent. Then she passed between two ringfires and was in the darkness again, running silently toward the thorn fence.

She reached the spot, praying to the Mother in her mind that it was not guarded. And whether by chance or the Mother's intervention, it was not. The cage hung high above the ground, too far for her to see anything within it. She looked around her, listened, sniffed the air in one last cautious attempt to ensure no one was nearby. As far as she could tell, no one was. She ran forward and began to climb nimbly, hand over hand, through the lower branches of the tree.

She stopped to get her bearings, then moved out onto the branch from which the cage was hung. Some instinct told her the little ogre knew she was there. But if so, he remained silent as ever.

"It is Shiva, little ogre," she whispered, just in case. She began to fumble with the knots that held the cage. "I am going to let you down. You must make no noise. When you reach the ground, I shall come down and let you out. Do you understand?"

Silence. No sound from the cage. Did he understand? Had he understood anything she had said to him from that moment when he had killed the wolf? No matter. She was here now. It was too late to turn back. "Make him stay quiet, Mother of All Things," she whispered in her mind.

The knots loosened suddenly, and for an instant she almost lost the cage as it began to slip down. But she caught the rope in time and held it looped so that she could lower the cage gradually rather than let it crash to the ground. Foot by foot she dropped it until at last the rope abruptly slackened. She sighed. Still no sound from the little ogre. That was good. She forced herself to sniff the wind and listen, but there was no one coming. Dark as it was, she ran the length of the branch and began to climb back down the tree.

A part of her mind was trying urgently to ask her questions. *What will they do? Will they find out? How will you—?* But she pushed all aside except the immediate problem.

Shiva reached the ground and scampered to the cage. The little ogre was in there all right: His scent was strong and, besides, she could see the huddled shadow on the cage floor. For some reason fear welled in her now that the final moment was upon her, and her hands grew large and awkward on the knots that shut the cage. Still no sound within, no hint of approaching guards, no indication anyone had seen her.

She had it! The ropes fell away and the cage door swung open with a tiny lattice creak.

"Come out!" whispered Shiva. She reached her

hand into the cage, toward the huddled shadow. "Come out! You must run! Run quickly before they find you!" *And find me*, she thought. If any knew that she had freed the ogre, she would be banished from the tribe.

There was a movement in the cage and the hairy boy, the little ogre, emerged timid as a nervous fawn.

"Run!" Shiva urged. "Run quickly!"

Watching from her smoke-filled cleft, the Crone's eyes glittered.

11
Hiram's Nightmare

Hiram dreamed. . . .

He stood before a great forest on a game trail. He was on the hunt, but the remainder of the hunters had deserted him. The track he followed disappeared into the gloomy depths.

The great forest closed around him, dark and threatening. Renka, the chief, walked beside him, urging him on. She had no fear of the forest, for women feared nothing.

"Will you tell me the game you hunt, Hiram?" she asked.

When he would not, for he was afraid to speak its name, she vanished, leaving him alone again.

The trail took him to a clearing and beyond the clearing a rise of cliffs, honeycombed with caves.

"You are forbidden the caves," Renka said.

"You must enter the caves," said a voice on his left side, the dry voice of the Crone. He looked around and above him and saw the Crone was flying with the forest spirits. She wore the skin of some great cat, which flapped behind her like wings.

He felt fear greater than he had ever felt before, fear that paralyzed his limbs. But he fought the fear because of the orders of the women. He stepped toward the cave mouth.

A monstrous shape rose up out of the ground before him, a beast in the form of a man, yet far more broadly built and muscular, hairy, with beetling brows and fearsome jaws. It stepped forward, arms wide to embrace him.

Hiram ran. He ran swifter than the deer or the sleek cats who hunt them. He ran swifter than a bird in flight.

He came upon a river and knew that if he followed the river, it must take him from the forest. But somehow he lost the river and was walking along the game trail, nose twitching. The fear was still strong in him.

A monstrous shape rose up before him.

Hiram ran again and was at the river and managed, somehow, to cross the river so that it was

92

between him and the creature that raged on the far bank. From the distance, he realized he had never seen anything more menacing, more ugly, more deadly, more frightening. It sought to catch him and open up his skull. But it could not cross water, so he was safe.

The forest thinned and he reached a second clearing in which grew a single tall tree. Hiram thought he would climb the tree and so find the path out of the deep forest. He moved toward it.

A monstrous shape rose up before him, arms outstretched to embrace him. Hiram turned to run, but the forest had closed in, tree ranked to tree, so that there was no escape. The huge arms closed around him, and the foul smell of the monster overpowered him.

Hiram woke.

He lay, heart pounding, drenched with sweat as the dream scent of the monster faded. But at once a new fear arose, pushing a lump of panic to his throat. He was in a strange chamber! He had been taken from the house of men! Then he remembered. He was to lead the hunt against the ogre clan and as leader had been given his own sleep shelter.

The ogre scent clung. It was far fainter, far more

distant than it had been in his dream, yet it remained. Hiram sat upright. His heartbeat had settled now, but he was nervously alert, unable to lie still. His nostrils twitched. Did he still smell the dream?

Cautiously he crawled from his shelter and stood upright. The village was illuminated brightly by the ringfires, and the air was full of woodsmoke, mingled with night smells. But the ogre scent remained.

Were ogres creeping up on the camp?

Hiram felt the fear he had experienced in the dream well up to overpower him. His life, his whole existence, had taken on a nightmarish quality. He was a hunter, a young hunter. He had never wished to lead the hunt, thinking himself too unskilled as yet, too inexperienced. Now he was to lead the hunt against the monsters of the deep caves. And suddenly the monsters, the ogres, were everywhere. He met them in his dreams, he smelled them on the night air.

He ran toward a ringfire where, as he had hoped, he found a guard, a thick-set woman by the name of Dreas, whose mate chipped spearheads for the hunt.

In his extremity, Hiram forgot his fear of women and actually dared to catch her by the arm. "Sniff the air, Dreas," he said urgently.

She peered into his face, frowning. "Hiram?"

"Yes, yes—it's Hiram. Will you—?"

Not all women were wise. Dreas blinked and said slowly, "You should be asleep, Hunter Hiram. You need your rest." She smiled suddenly, almost proudly. "You lead the hunt for the monsters tomorrow!" The smile faded. "You need your rest, Hunter Hiram." She reached out and cuffed him on the ear, not angrily, but with enough force to sting.

Hiram reeled away, more from surprise than anything else, but recovered at once and moved forward to take her arm again. "Dreas, listen to me!" he hissed.

"No need to worry, Hiram," Dreas said. She gestured with her free hand. "See, the ringfires are high. Nothing can harm you. Dreas is on guard."

Hiram shook her. "Sniff the air!" he screamed. She was broader than he and probably stronger, but he shook her until her teeth rattled.

Dreas stared at him in blank amazement. Eventually she said, "Sniff the air?"

"Yes!" Hiram urged. "Yes! Yes!" He himself sniffed, exaggeratedly, to demonstrate. The accursed smell of ogre was still on the wind, faint, distant, but definite.

Dreas sniffed cautiously, watching Hiram. Women were the leaders of the tribe. Men treated them with deference and respect: the elders in the first rank, but after them all women. Men shouted only at each other, never at women. "I sniff," she said. Her eyes were very wary, as if she expected Hiram to attack her. He noticed she had tightened her grip on her spear.

"What do you smell?"

"Woodsmoke," Dreas told him promptly.

"Yes, yes—and what else?"

Dreas sniffed again. "I smell hyena," she said. She looked at him anxiously, as if for approval.

"Yes—hyena. Yes, what else?"

Dreas sniffed again. Very gently she removed her arm from his hand. She smiled, uncertainly, like a child discovering the rules of a strange new game. "Leopard? Do you smell leopard, Hiram?"

"Yes, leopard and wolf—but what else?"

"Why are you angry, Hiram?" She frowned more deeply. "And why are you impolite?"

"I'm not angry, Dreas. Please, I'm not angry. I'm not impolite. Please, Lady Dreas, try to concentrate. *What else do you smell?*"

She shrugged. "Nothing."

"You don't smell . . ." He half swallowed the word in his panicked attempt to get it out, ". . . ogre?"

"Yes."

"You do?"

"Yes."

Hiram reached for her again, but she stepped back quickly and eluded his grasp. "Why didn't you say?" he asked her.

"I thought you meant *outside*," Dreas said accusingly. "The ogre smell is *inside*. That little monster has been stinking up the camp ever since they put it in the cage."

"No, Dreas, I didn't me—" He stopped. The little ogre! That was it! That was what he smelled—the ogre cub in the cage. Of course! How could he have been so stupid!

He swallowed hard and began to back away. "Thank you, Dreas. I'm sorry. Thank you. Yes. The cub. Thank you. I'm sorry."

She watched him silently, with a mixed expression of sadness and incredulity.

Hiram returned to his shelter. Why? Why did he do this to himself? Every day of his life, it seemed, he discovered a new way to make himself look foolish before women.

Hiram froze in the process of crawling back into his shelter. The little ogre was hanging caged to the *south* of the camp. The scent he picked up on the wind was faint, but he was sure it came from the *west*. He sniffed again. Yes, he was certain.

For a long while, Hiram remained where he was. His mind ran around in undecided circles. There was definitely something to the west. He sniffed again. The wind had changed so that he could no longer smell it, but that did not matter. There was something to the west.

But what to do?

He dared not alert the guards. Not now, not after making such a fool of himself before Dreas. He could not risk humiliating himself again. He would have to make certain.

He slid into the shelter to look for his spear, then remembered it was still by his old place in the house of men. All he had here was a half-chipped ax he had planned to finish working in the morning. He stared at it with heavy heart. It was not much, but he supposed it was better than nothing and stuck it in his tawny belt. He probably wouldn't need it anyway, he reassured himself glumly. The smell was probably not an ogre smell at all. The number of mistakes he had been making lately, it was more likely something else altogether. A hedgehog, perhaps. A hedgehog with fleas.

He slipped from the shelter and, taking care to avoid Dreas, moved quickly to the western part of the camp. The wind was blowing from the north now, so there was still no confirmation of the smell.

He reached the thorn fence and skirted it, pleased to find it unbroken. He waited until the guard left the westernmost ringfire, then scampered quickly past it and through the small gap it guarded.

He was outside the fence now, but still within the ring of firelight, still safe. Hiram tugged the half-finished axhead from his belt and moved to the outer edge of the ring of light. At first he could see nothing beyond, in the darkness. Then a monstrous shape rose up before him, arms outstretched.

12

Flight from the Village

"Go *on*," whispered Shiva. But the little ogre would not go.

Behind them she could hear a sudden commotion in the village camp: a woman's voice shouting, then answering shouts almost at once from both women and men. She was discovered! But how could she be discovered? It did not matter. The village was awake now, and if she was not discovered, it was only a matter of time.

"Shoo!" She made sweeping gestures with both arms, as one might do to frighten away an animal, but still the little ogre did not move. "Oh please," Shiva gasped. "Please go away! They'll find us soon and they'll put you in the cage again!" Or worse, her mind suggested. The discussions had gone on all day: how and how soon to kill the ogre cub.

Everyone was agreed he should be killed. The only discussion was on the method and the time.

The little ogre was watching her intently, slumped in that peculiar crouching stance of his. Then, slowly, without change of expression, he held one hand out toward her, trusting as a child.

"No!" Shiva gasped. She closed her eyes. "Oh, no, I *can't*! I can't come with you!" Behind them the commotion was growing louder with more shouting and the sound of running footsteps. She opened her eyes and the hand was still there, reaching for her own.

Time froze into an immobile moment. She looked into the deep brown eyes, soft as the eyes of aurochs cattle. She looked at the outstretched hand. The sounds behind were sounds of pursuit, loud and angry.

They would put him back in the cage.

They would kill him. He had saved her from the wolf and they would kill him.

Nothing—nothing of importance—ever happens by accident.

They would kill him. They would kill him. They would kill him!

The moment shattered. Shiva took the outstretched hand. "Come on!" She tugged and ran.

They ran together into the night, away from the uproar in the village.

Shiva reached the river and followed it, stumbling in the darkness, until she found the spot where the river narrowed and a fallen tree provided a means to cross. It was not easy to negotiate, even in daylight, but she did not know what else to do. The sounds of pursuit had fallen behind, but she did not imagine she had lost them yet. She might evade the tribe's hunters at night—for a while, if she was lucky—but in the morning, in the daylight, they would find their track. Once that happened, it was only a matter of time. Unless . . .

"We have to cross the river," she told the little ogre. She pointed, without knowing if he understood, then removed her hand from his. She needed both hands free to negotiate the crossing and could only hope he would follow her. "Cross the river," she said again, then, before her fear could build, climbed onto the fallen tree.

It was hard going. Several times she came perilously close to tumbling into the water, and she was forced to move so slowly it drove her half mad with frustration. When she calculated she was about halfway across, she jammed herself into the fork of a thick branch and looked back.

There was no sign of the little ogre. She held her

breath and listened, desperately searching for any sound above the roar of the river. There was none.

The sliverlike moon appeared abruptly from behind a cloud and she saw him, a solid crouching shape, still on the bank.

"Come on!" Shiva called quietly, fearful that the pursuing hunters might hear. "You have to follow me!"

He remained immobile. She could not even tell if he had heard her, did not know if he could even see her. Should she go back for him? But if she went back for him, what could she do? She had found it difficult enough to get this far with both hands free. If she took his hand again and tried to cross while dragging him, she might kill them both.

"Little ogre!" she called, louder this time. "You must come quickly!"

For a moment more he remained immobile, then, quite suddenly, he leaped onto the tree bridge and swarmed across, hand over hand, with the sure-footed ease of a monkey. He arrived beside her in a fraction of the time she had taken. To her amazement, he threw his arms around her neck and nuzzled her cheek.

"Yes, I like you too," Shiva said, extricating herself with difficulty. "But we have to get to the other side." She began to move again, cautiously, with great difficulty, and was mortified when he climbed past her and ran the remaining distance. He was squatting on the far bank waiting for her when she arrived. "Come on," Shiva said sourly. She half turned away from him, but he held out his hand as he had done before. She stared at it for a moment, then broke into a smile. "All right," she said. "All right." She took his hand.

They trotted along the far bank, following the course of the river until Shiva found what she was searching for: a shallow tributary stream. She stopped for a moment, listening, but the noise of the water made it quite impossible to determine how close the pursuit had come. She shrugged. No matter. If they could only keep ahead just a little longer, there was a good chance they could elude the hunt. She tugged his hand and stepped into the water.

The little ogre would not come. Caught off balance, Shiva almost fell as she jerked to a halt.

"What's wrong?"

He released her hand and sat down, a stubborn expression on his face. They were only a foot or two away from one another, but that expression told her they were abruptly worlds apart.

"What's wrong?" she asked again. She glanced behind him for signs of the hunters, but could see nothing. "Don't be difficult, little ogre. We have to go this way." Which was true. The only sure way of outwitting the hunt was to walk in water. It carried away your scent and wiped out your tracks.

The little ogre stared at her, saying nothing.

"We *have* to!" said Shiva desperately. "It's shallow—you won't drown—see?" She walked to the very center of the stream, which flowed no higher than her knees.

The little ogre stayed where he was.

Shiva waded back to the edge. "Listen to me," she said in sudden anger. "This is your fault. I didn't want to come out here at night. I let you loose because you killed the wolf, so now we're even. But if you're too stupid to—" She half wondered if it would be possible to make her way back to the camp, to creep in unnoticed as she had done a hundred times before.

What she was saying was true. They *were* even now. He had saved her life by killing the wolf and she had saved his by releasing him from the cage. It could stop there. He was free of the cage and out of the camp and ahead of the hunters. For the moment at least.

She sighed. It was no good. She stepped out of the stream, gripped his shoulders and shook him. "Come on! You're going to get us into so much trouble—"

He remained quite passive beneath her hands,

the ugly great head bobbing loosely as she shook him. She let go and walked back into the stream, moving determinedly against the flow, in the hope that he would follow, as he had on the bridge. She stopped and looked back. The moon was out again and she could see he had not moved.

She waded back and stood looking at him. She felt like screaming, but instead she held out her hand. After a long moment he took it and waded after her into the stream.

It was obvious he loathed water, but he stayed with her as she turned and twisted from one stream branch to another. Eventually she was satisfied and led him out. They moved away from the water, stopped and listened, sniffing the air. She heard nothing, scented nothing, sensed no pursuit. Relief flooded through her and suddenly she was very tired.

"Come on," she said again, tugging the hairy hand in hers.

They slept in the safety of a high tree, which he climbed more easily than she did. When she found a secure platform of branches and lay down, he came to her and put his arms around her and snuggled close, falling asleep almost at once. She tried to wriggle away, but he was amazingly strong. His grip was tight and she did not really want to wake him. So she lay, seeking sleep herself. At first his scent disturbed her, but after a time she grew accustomed to it. There were no sounds below other than the usual night sounds. Eventually, lulled by his body heat, she too slept.

She awoke alone at dawn, muscles stiff, with blood dried on a cut across her forearm that had gone unnoticed the night before. As always, she awoke completely, very aware of herself and her surroundings. Where was the little ogre?

The tree stood solitary on the edge of sweeping grassland. Behind her, to the south, was an area of rock and shrub. Beyond that, more trees and the network of streams leading to the river on the far horizon. The camp was out of sight, but not nearly as far distant as she had imagined last night in the darkness. They would have to move on and move quickly. Where was the little ogre?

To the west, she could see the stand of trees that marked the edges of the forest, an area shunned by the tribe as spirit-ridden and dangerous. Eastward, the plain swung around in a series of dips and hollows before reaching that same range of cliffs against which the village camp was pitched farther down. Where would they go?

The night before, Shiva had acted on impulse and instinct, without real thought. Now, in the chill

107

dawn, she faced the consequences. She was a fugitive from her tribe and, by all appearances, little mother to an ogre child. They would need food. They would need shelter. And they would need to find somewhere they could hide from the tribe. All quickly. Where was he?

She heard a small sound directly below her and reached instinctively for the flint knife in her belt. But then the little ogre swung up onto the platform of branches. In one hand he was carrying something wrapped in a broad leaf. In the other was the skinned carcass of a small animal, partly eaten. He handed both across.

To her astonishment, she recognized the animal as a young wildcat, a dangerous and difficult prey. The spine was severed at the neck, with prominent teeth marks around the wound, so presumably he had killed it the same way he killed the wolf. She disliked cat meat, especially raw, but was impressed by the kill. The hunt seldom returned with cat of any sort, preferring easier prey. Perhaps the little ogre would not need so much looking after as she had thought.

She opened the leaf and discovered a writhing collection of grubs and ants, a far more suitable breakfast.

She finished the last of the grubs and threw away

the leaf. Then, using a creeper, she tied together the hind legs of the wildcat carcass and strung it from her belt. As she did so, it occurred to her that the little ogre, who had seemed ignorant of the way to skin a wolf, had managed to skin the wildcat very effectively. Had he learned by watching her? Or had he known all along? And with what had he skinned the cat? He carried no knife or axe.

Where should they go? She started to make her way down the tree, half an eye cast toward the growing thunderheads. Soon it would rain. That was nothing in itself, but it reminded her of what they needed and in what order. Even in the spring-time, with the days lengthening and warming, they could not go on sleeping in trees. They needed shelter and somewhere to hide from the hunters.

It occurred to her that she actually knew how to make a shelter. It was only a question of wood frame, branches and mud, and there was no need to build a large one since it was needed only to house the little ogre and herself. But then that curious pictorial aspect of her mind showed her quite suddenly that such a solitary shelter would never do.

Where to go? She reached the ground and noted with satisfaction that the little ogre was climbing down after her. If he stayed close and followed without her having to urge or drag him, life would be very much easier. But where to go?

She watched the little ogre reach the ground and drop into his accustomed crouch, watching her. Where had he come from? What was he doing near the tribal camp? Did he too have a tribe? Did he have parents, a mother and a father? Or was he an orphan also?

For some reason the thought saddened her greatly, forcing her mind back on her own situation. She had lost her father before she was even born, her mother not long after. Now she had lost her tribe as well, for she knew that once they had discovered she had freed the little ogre, banishment must be the least of her punishments. Father, mother, tribe—all gone from her now, leaving her alone with this strange little creature from the ca—

The caves! Was it possible they could take shelter in the caves! The thought struck her with extraordinary force. Caves were forbidden to the tribe. Or rather wrapped around with endless rules. Certain caves near the campsites were traditionally reserved for tribal dignitaries: the Keeper of the Drums, the Crone, the Mixer of the Paints. Other deep caves were reserved to store the winter meat.

But all other caves were shunned as dangerous. If they were not home to animals like the lion or cave bear, they might be home to monsters like the nightwing, or the haunt of spirits who would eat your soul. For this reason, every woman, every man, every child of the tribe was forbidden by the elders to enter a strange cave in groups of less than five, and even then with care.

They would never think to look for her in the caves! But dare she shelter there? She stared at the little ogre. Ogres were reputed to live in caves. The ogre boy with her now might have lived his entire life in one. If he dared, why not she?

The thought frightened and attracted her. If she overcame her fear, she would have to select the cave with great care, of course. The elders did not forbid the caves on whim: The dangers were real enough. But if she found a cave and approached it carefully, slowly, with infinite patience, her nose must tell her if it contained lion or bear. And if she watched and listened and *sensed* the world around her, surely she could tell if there were spirits? And if she chose a shallow cave, it was unlikely there would be monsters, for everyone knew the monsters favored deep caves.

Dared she do it? The right cave, well positioned, difficult to reach, would be safe from prowling cats or other beasts of prey. It would be a perfect shelter from the wind and rain. It would be warm, for could she not light a fire? And best of all, it would be the one place no hunter would ever think to look. But dared she do it? The thought excited her greatly, yet in her heart of hearts she knew she could not. However much sense it made, she could never find the courage to face what might be waiting in the caves.

Was there another way? Was there another place to go to?

She was so wrapped in her thoughts, she did not even see the rhino until it had begun its charge.

13

Thag Triumphant

Hana watched the clearing from the cave mouth. Hagar squatted beside her, absently toying with a pebble, half worked into a tiny axhead by one of the children. Early sunlight filtered through the forest canopy, casting a rich, green glow as if the clan lived underwater.

Below, in the clearing, the first of the women were stirring, beginning their morning collection of firewood and water. Later there would be more of them, gathered to cut strips from old meat and talk among themselves. Later still, the men would appear, scratching themselves, arguing and seeking food.

"Where are they?" Hana asked, as much to herself as her companion.

But Hagar elected to answer. "They will come soon," he whispered.

She watched a young woman, scarcely more than a girl and only recently mated, cross the clearing with a light, easy step. She carried a pot hollowed from a length of wooden log and was obviously heading for the stream.

"What will happen, Hagar?" Hana asked him softly. She shivered, as if she already had an answer and was fearful of it.

"They will bring back Doban," Hagar said with inflated confidence. "And punish the Weakling Strangers," he added. But his voice was less firm when he said this and he did not meet her eyes.

Hana gestured at the girl with the pot. "We have hidden from the Weakling Strangers since my grandmother was no older than that child," she said bluntly. "How shall we punish them now?"

"Thag is strong," Hagar told her piously. "The strongest of the clan—the strongest of *any* clan. He will—"

"He will bellow and roar and frighten children," Hana interrupted sourly, able to speak freely in her love for Thag and in her confidence that Hagar loved him too. "Will you not tell me the truth, Hagar? You have wisdom. Will you not share it with me?"

"There is fear in my heart, Hana," Hagar whispered.

"And in mine," said Hana, her eyes back on the clearing. The cliff face rose steep and sheer beneath her, pocked with caves and caverns that formed a vast interlocking warren. There was an easy entrance hidden by a bush near the forest floor, but some clan members preferred to climb the cliff face.

"They will return with Doban," Hagar predicted. "You need have no fear of that, Hana. Heft the Hunter said he was hung in a cage from a tree branch. Those of the clan climb better than a leopard, and Thag will tear apart the cage."

After a long moment, Hana asked, "Why is there fear in your heart, Hagar?"

He remained silent for so long, she thought he would not answer her, but eventually he spoke.

"Because it will not end there," Hagar whispered.

Hana nodded slowly. *No*, she thought, *it will not end there*. Men like Thag might beat their chests and threaten, but all knew that concealment was the only real protection from the Weakling Strangers. The clans had hidden for generations, keeping to the forests and the deep caves, so that the Strangers had come to believe they did not exist at all. But when Doban was captured, they had living proof.

"They will come after us?" Hana asked.

Hagar nodded. "It is their way. It has always been their way."

"They would not dare enter the deep forest," Hana muttered, though she did not completely believe it.

"They would dare," Hagar said. "Now that they know we are here, they will enter the deep forest. They will hunt us, and if they find us they will seek to kill us." He leaned forward and dropped the toy axhead so that it tumbled down from the cave mouth to the clearing below. Watching it fall, he added, "They will seek to kill us all."

"Even the children?"

Hagar wrapped both arms around her close so that she might draw comfort from his body heat. "Especially the children, little sister," he whispered. "They hate us and they fear us, so they do not seek to conquer us—they seek to kill us and all our generations."

How, Hagar wondered, could any living creature embody such evil as the Strangers? Even the leopard killed only for food. "Will they venture into the deep caves?" she asked Hagar.

He unwound his arms from about her and stared thoughtfully out across the clearing, his eyes wandering through the upper terraces of the forest. "They may be afraid to enter the caves."

116

"Afraid?"

"We of the clans see better than the Strangers in the dark. Thus, in the deep caves, we have an advantage over them. Besides, they believe spirits and monsters live in caves."

What an odd belief. Her eye caught a movement in the forest on the edge of the clearing, but it was only a bird dropping down to take a berry from a bush. Where are they?

"So we may be safe if we retreat to the deep caves?"

"Thag is chief," Hagar said carefully. "He will decide such things." She was about to interrupt, but he pressed on without a pause, "It would be safe to hide in the deep caves, for if they did not know us to be there, I do not think they would enter and search. But if they saw us go into them, they would follow. And if we did anything to make them angry, they would surely search."

Would they never come? Thag had led his small raiding party out of the caves the night before. He was calm then and well drilled both by Hagar and by Heft the Hunter. The plan was one of stealth, not strength. They would move in the darkness, confident of their superior night vision. Heft would lead them to the place where Doban was caged. Heft did not think there would be guards, for he had seen none before, but if there were guards, or if there were Strangers near, they would wait. Hagar and Heft had together created a plan, "for the sake of the boy," and Thag, who was like clay in their hands when they mentioned the boy, had agreed. They would wait. Only when there were no Strangers would they rescue Doban.

But a plan was one thing and patience another. If Hana closed her eyes, she could see her massive mate impatient in the darkness, breathing through his nose as a bull snorts, unable to curb himself, Strangers or no Strangers. Thag liked Heft and respected him greatly, but he would not be held for long. He would want to act.

What could we do that would make them angry? she heard herself ask Hagar only a moment before. *Only kill some of their number? Oh Thag, my mate, have you killed by now? Have you brought the wrath of the Strangers upon us?*

As if he had read her thought, Hagar murmured, "It is the plan that makes them late."

"You think—?" She stopped. There was something approaching through the forest, something large, uncaring of who heard it. She stood up and pushed past Hagar without a word, almost running through the cave and into the dark passages that interconnected through the cliff face. Any stranger who blundered into this maze would have been lost within minutes, but Hana turned and twisted through the passages and tunnels with thoughtless confidence.

She emerged out of the entrance on the forest floor as Thag burst into the clearing. He was obviously excited, his eyes glowing with that wild inner fire that had attracted her so much when they were young, but beyond that, she could tell nothing. She saw at once that Doban was not with him.

"Eeeeeaaaaah!" roared Thag in a voice that echoed through the forest like the bellow of a mammoth. "Come down! Come out the clan—your chief has returned!" He stood up tall, waving both arms in the air, his hands curled into fists. Hana's heart sank. It was his victory stance. In a moment, if the excitement overpowered him, he would begin to dance. But victory meant battle and battle meant the death of Strangers and if the Strangers were angry . . .

She strode across the clearing. "Where is Doban?" she demanded sharply. "Have you brought back my son?"

"Our son," Thag growled. He stared at her for a moment, brown eyes glinting, then threw back his head and roared again, "Come out the clan!"

"Never mind 'Come out the clan'!" Hana spat. "You will tell me what happened. At once!"

He pushed his huge face close to hers, eyes glinting. "I am strong," he warned her. "The strongest of the clan." One huge hand reached out, finger pointed to stab her on the shoulder. "You will have patience, woman, because I, Thag, your husband and your chief, have much to say and I shall say it to the whole clan!"

She turned her head and snapped at his finger with strong teeth so that he withdrew it quickly with a tiny whimper. "Why did you do that?" he asked her in a furious whisper.

Hana stepped so close that she almost touched his chest, holding him with her eyes. "Where is Doban?" she asked. "Where is Doban, Thag?"

She could feel the pressure of the clan building up behind her as more and more emerged from the caves. Soon it would be too late. He would be the chief who addressed his people, and she would have to wait through some prolonged and windy speech to find out what had really happened.

"Ah-ha!" Thag said infuriatingly. He straightened to look over her head across the assembled clan. He raised his right arm high into the air, slowly curled his hand into a massive fist, which he brought down to thump his broad chest with a resounding thud.

"I, Thag, strongest of the clan, led my warriors to the camp of the Weakling Strangers!"

There was a ragged growl of approval that fell short of becoming a cheer.

"Get on! Get on!" murmured Hana, but softly, for she had no wish to stop him getting to the point. It was not all bad. Even if Doban was not rescued, it could not be all bad. His mood was wrong. She had to be patient, even though it galled her. He would ramble and boast, but he would tell it all eventually. And it would not be all bad.

"In the darkness we went, when the weak eyes of the Weakling Strangers could not see us. We crept to their filthy, smelly camp like the lioness who stalks her prey! We went to rescue my son, Doban!"

This time there was a cheer, although all in the clan had known about the raid and its purpose the day before. Let them cheer about results, thought Hana, but she said nothing.

Thag·stared across his clan, eyes darting from one individual to another. "We of the clan are stronger than the Strangers. Stronger, wiser and more handsome. We are bigger, better hunters. We are more favored by our ancestors and the gods. We have more hair! Yet we left the Strangers alone, for we have always wished to live in peace. Yet these same Strangers, without cause or reason, stole my son!"

121

"Our son," Hana murmured.

"Should that crime go unpunished?" Thag bellowed.

"*No!*" roared the gathered clan.

Hana's heart sank at the word *punished*. He had killed a Stranger—perhaps more than one. She stared intently at his face, trying to read it. But all she could see there was elation and the glow that always came when he addressed the clan.

"No!" Thag roared back. "And it did not go unpunished. We went to the Strangers' camp, I, Thag, and Thonar and Mabango and Heft the Hunter, all of us with stealth and cunning in the night. They feared our coming, for they had great fires burning, even though wood is scarce for them because they will not enter our forest. They placed many, many guards, but we evaded them easily, for they were all stupid and some of them were women. We crept close to the camp."

He was beginning to relive the recollection as those of the clan so often did, watching pictures in his head, for there, before the assembled clan, he began to creep about as he had crept toward the Strangers' camp.

"We sniffed the air, in search of my son Doban." He sniffed the air in an exaggerated parody. "My friend Heft the Hunter, greatest tracker of the clans, knew they had put him in a cage." He stopped, looked around, then repeated explosively, "The Weakling Strangers *caged my son!*"

There was an outbreak of snarls and growls behind Hana, all from the men, of course; the women, as always, listened more sensibly.

"But we have exacted our revenge!" roared Thag. His control broke and he did indeed dance with excitement, stamping his feet on the forest floor, tossing his head and jerking his body spasmodically. He plunged momentarily into the crowd, which scattered before him.

Revenge . . . the word echoed through Hana's mind like the final rattle of a dying man. Had he killed? He must have killed.

Thag stopped, turned, straightened and strode dramatically to the exact center of the clearing. He struck a heroic pose, head back, and flung out one great arm. "See!" he roared. "See what we have brought!"

Doban! Hana thought, her earlier concerns blown away like smoke. *He has brought Doban!*

Thonar and Mabango emerged from the forest, dragging a smaller shape between them. But it was not Doban. It was a skin-clad, wide-eyed, hairless Weakling Stranger who looked as though he walked within the most terrifying nightmare of his life.

14
Drums of War

The preparation for war began with a drumbeat, moments before dawn. The sound reverberated dully through the camp, slow and deliberate like a giant heart. It was a calling; and the tribe began to gather. All knew what must be done.

There was the smell of rain on the air, although it had been dry for several days. And when the sun rose, it rose over towering cloud formations with that dirty pinkish hue that threatened rain or even snow. They watched the dawn in total silence, broken by the slow, relentless drumbeat.

The elders emerged from the longhouse, where they had been meeting through the latter part of the night. They had donned their ancient ceremonial dress, hide and feathers dyed yellow, red and purple with the juice of plants. Renka, the chief, wore the skin of a cave lioness pulled forward to form a hood that hid a portion of her face. She carried a staff surmounted by a feline skull.

Moving with stately grace, she led the elders in a complete circuit of the village, ending in the central clearing where all such rituals were carried out. The faces of the elders were solemn.

There was a platform of rough wood set to the west of the longhouse and surmounted by a massive wooden log. Renka climbed to sit upon it so that she was head and shoulders above the rest, who stood. She stared out, reading expectation on their faces. She struck the platform by her feet with the butt of her wooden staff.

Renka waited.

There was a shuffling sound as the first of the warrior men appeared, hunters all, but now without the tawny girdle of their rank. A score or more of them trotted to the space before the platform and stood, muffled in their pelts and furs against the chill of dawn. None armed. Not one carried so much as a flint knife for skinning.

The drumbeat sounded, slow and steady. None could see the hidden drummer or the hidden drum.

A steady, trilling ululation emerged from the longhouse, like the call of a wild bird. It hung for a moment, sweet and pure on the morning air, then died. The warriors began to remove their furs and skins.

In a moment they stood almost naked in the clearing, holding themselves straight and immobile despite the chilling winds. The wailing came again, shorter this time and more shrill. Six young women emerged from the longhouse, moving to the drumbeat, carrying small pots fashioned from the skulls of rodents. Their heads bobbed up and down, like the heads of birds. Six more emerged, older than the first. Each carried in her left hand a bundle of cut reeds, and rushes in her right.

The drumbeat quickened almost imperceptibly. Dipping their reeds and rushes into the contents of the pots, the women began to paint the naked bodies of the men. Streaks of crimson and vermilion, whorls of deep blue, designs of yellow ocher, rings of emerald, spots of purple crushed from berries. In the chill wind, the paints and dyes dried almost at once. The women worked quickly, expertly, painting from foot to neck. They stood back.

As one, the men began to move, shaking their bodies and stamping their feet. Some turned full circle on their heels, moving to the quickened rhythm of the hidden drum.

The drum stopped and the men, dressed again, froze back into their former immobility. The women moved forward at once and smeared their faces with thin clay that dried gray-white, giving them a fearsome, deathlike look. When they had finished, the men raised a brief, deep, coughing cheer, like the sound the leopard makes before a kill, and trotted off.

At once a second group of warrior men appeared, running with loping gait into the clearing to stop and bow before the waiting women. They tore off their furs and pelts more roughly than the first group and the painting began anew.

The process was repeated time and time again until every male warrior in the tribe had been suitably adorned. The women withdrew to the longhouse, carrying their empty pots.

There was silence for a moment, then the drum began again, tapping out a different rhythm, far faster and more complex. The warrior women came then, dressed more lightly than the men since women bore the cold with greater fortitude. Several elders stood among them, for these were the leaders of the tribe. What could be seen of their bodies, except for the faces, showed blue, dyed, but not painted. They drew up in ranks before the platform of the chief.

The painters returned with fresh pots that contained only the red ocher called the Mother's blood and the milk-white sap pressed from the stem of a river fern. With these paints and their fingers, they began to create intricate designs on the faces of the warrior women. The white sap went on first, like a base, then lines of red and blocks of red and streaks of red until the women's faces became the faces of demons. A young girl with a new pot came then and painted the lips of the warrior women so deep a blue that they seemed black.

A shout went up from the assembled tribe, and the warrior men returned, jostling and shouting, to mingle with the warrior women. Together they were a fearsome sight, like an army of corpses led by devils.

Again the drumming changed its beat and an old, old man appeared, moving in strict time to the rhythm, three steps forward, two steps back. He held a flint block in one hand, a strikestone in the other. As he danced, he struck the flint, expertly removing slim bladed flakes. All knew him. His name was Nagek and in his day he had been the greatest of all the weapons craftsmen. Even now, extreme age seemed to have robbed him of little of his skill, only his speed and stamina.

Behind Nagek, moving in the same three-forward-two-back rhythm, came a score of young people, scarcely more than children, boys and girls both, and all carrying weapons: bone- and flint-tipped spears, long-bladed knives of fine-edged flint, clubs of bone and wood, throwing sticks, throwing stones gathered from a half-forgotten shore, smooth polished by the waters.

The cavalcade halted eventually before the assembled warriors and laid down the weapons in a great heap only a few yards away. No one moved.

The solitary drumbeat changed texture and was joined by other hidden drums. They began to beat in a curious counterpoint that reached out to tweak the human heartbeat and create an air of solemn expectation. The sounds rose steadily in the morning air, then stopped.

In the silence came a chilling sound close at hand: the coughing roar of a hunting panther.

Then, on silent, padding feet, the catmen came.

They came together, dressed in their appropriate skins, initiates of the Leopard Lodge, the Panther Lodge, the Lodge of Lynx, the Lodge of Lion. Their bodies, near naked despite the cold, were dyed or painted striped or spotted in imitation of the cats they honored. Their eyes peered out from beneath the cats' heads of the captured pelts. Each man carried a whisk and a small but brimming pot. The pots smelled of fresh blood.

They circled the weapons pile with great deliberation. On the third circuit, they dipped their whisks into their pots and flicked them toward the pile, spraying the weapons with the blood. Those of the tribe who watched sighed deeply. Blood magic was potent. Soon these same weapons would run with ogre blood.

Suddenly the pots and whisks were set aside, the drums erupted into a far faster rhythm and the catmen began a violent, leaping dance, spitting and growling, making raking motions at each other with outstretched, clawlike hands. A young boy ran among them, scampering swiftly on all fours, and they fell upon him as cats fall on their prey. The boy went down with a realistic scream and was carried off, arms and legs outstretched, head rolling as if dead.

Once, thought Renka, the boy really would have been killed. But they had discovered the magic still worked without this sacrifice, so there was no longer any need to deplete the tribe.

She glanced to the east and saw the sun had fully risen now, although it was partially obscured by growing clouds. The Mother was kind. Soon there would be rain, and the rain would wash away their scent and the monsters would not smell them coming.

Renka stood abruptly, jumping nimbly from the

platform, and strode toward the weapons pile. She was a short, somewhat stocky woman, unskilled with spears but very strong in the arms, so she selected a stout wooden club. An excited cheer arose as she held it high; then the painted warriors, men and women both, fell upon the pile to select their own weapons.

The arming of the warriors triggered a distinct air of expectation. A rippling, subdued murmur that was almost an unease passed through the entire tribe. Renka herself felt uneasy.

Was she doing the right thing? Before, when the elder council had decided what action to take and appointed Hiram to lead the warriors, they had planned little more than a raid, something designed to hunt a few ogres perhaps, but more to warn them, frighten them away, ensure they kept their distance.

What was happening now was very different. It was preparation for a full-scale war. And war at a level the tribe had not experienced in generations. The plan, quite simply, was to search out the ogre clan and attack with such ferocity that the threat was totally eliminated.

What option was there for the tribe? The ogres had raided in the night. Now Hiram and the orphan Shiva were missing. No bodies had been found, so it was likely the ogres had carried them off. Every-one knew ogres preferred human meat to any other.

We caged their cub, a small voice whispered in her mind. *We planned to kill it. They did no more than we would have done had they stolen one of ours.*

Was it right what she did? Was it right what she planned? The elders were behind her without res-ervation. But the Crone . . .

Somehow she could not quite understand the Crone. The woman had emerged from her spirit cave only an hour before the dawn and joined in the deliberations of the council when they were almost done.

Did the Crone approve their plan? Renka did not know. But she did not disapprove. Was she not prepared to lend her magic?

As if in answer to the thought, a great, low rum-bling sound like nearby thunder broke over the camp. She knew what it was at once, as did every other member of the tribe. She heard the voice of "the big cow," largest of the herd of *koma* drums. The hair on the back of Renka's neck prickled.

The komana initiates came then, men and women, their bodies and faces painted starkly, black on white, the pelts they wore stained white. Leading their procession was the giant Runar, a man so huge he might himself have been an ogre, towering head and shoulders above any other in the tribe, one powerful arm encircling "the big cow" while his other hand beat out the rhythm.

Behind Runar walked Sheena, keeper of the Sacred Drums, mother of Hiram, graying now, her set face speaking of the worry that lay heavy on her. Renka's heart went out to her. Hiram was her only child. *Had been* her only child, for surely if the ogres took him, he could no longer be alive.

The tribe fell absolutely silent. Only at a time of utmost importance was the herd displayed, only when they wished to signal the attention of the Mother of All Things were the *dikomana* played. They were potent magic for a time when such magic was sorely needed.

The white-clad figures formed a tight circle, Runar at its central point, and began to play the Sacred Drums in earnest then.

The sound went on and on, growing imperceptibly until it filled the entire camp and stretched beyond, rolling toward the far horizon, rolling upward like the smoke of ringfires, rolling out beyond the clouds, beyond the sky until it reached the dreamtime and the Mother's ears. . . .

It stopped.

Into the clearing, with a bloodcurdling shriek,

leaped a nightmare figure, dressed head to foot in the skin of a cave bear, face blackened beneath the massive skull, gripping a rattle in one hand, a horsetail whisk in the other.

The *dikomana* started up again at once, a fast beat that built quickly to a frenzy while the figure leaped and twisted in a grotesque spirit-dance, which sent tribespeople scattering each time it came near.

Renka marveled as the skin was hurled aside to reveal the wizened, white-haired Crone beneath, eyes vacant, jaw slack, possessed utterly by those spirits who hurled her ancient body back and forth with wild abandon.

The tribe watched, half petrified, as the Crone became, in turn, a lumbering bear, a stalking cat, a charging bull, a slithering snake. Then some elemental force took hold of her and blazed behind her eyes. She walked, head high now, with a stately, brittle pace that swept all before it, hands fluttering lightly in a movement that forced the mind to think of snow. The Crone had become Mamar, God of Ice, and the tribe wondered at so great a miracle.

The force died and was replaced by a procession of ancestral spirits who spoke through her mouth and uttered prophecies in strange spirit tongues.

And when the ancestral spirits had gone, there came at length one who stared out through the Crone's eyes and raised the Crone's head and beckoned.

It was time.

Renka stepped forward and felt the rest of the elder council fall in step behind her. The crowd parted, then followed, silently, a respectful distance behind. All knew where they were going, all feared the thing that was to be done.

The Crone walked purposefully, quickly beyond the longhouse, beyond the house of women, beyond the shelters, beyond the dying ringfires to the towering cliff. The body of the tribe halted here, for it was forbidden that they should go farther. But the Crone strode on to disappear without a moment's hesitation into a large and lowering cave mouth.

Renka and the elders entered the cave. It was a huge, gloomy cavern, large enough to soak up the light so that its roof could not be seen. There was no sign of the Crone, but they knew the way and walked diagonally until they reached an opening in the far left wall and entered a narrow passage.

It was difficult going, even with the torches, and Renka wondered—not for the first time—how the Crone, older by far than any of them, had managed in total darkness. But then, she reminded herself, it was only the body of the Crone that was old and frail; the spirit within was different now, the spirit of the Mother of All Things.

The passage plunged downward, became more narrow still so that they were forced to move in single file. The torches guttered and flickered and threatened to go out. They reached a short stretch comprising several natural steps and emerged into a long gallery that led to a second tunnel, wider and flatter than the first, but twisting so that sense of direction became utterly confused. The tunnel opened onto a narrow ledge that ran alongside a drop of almost thirty feet. Renka shuffled forward, holding tight to her emotions, then thankfully entered another passage. They were almost at their destination.

The final passage ran straight and true and opened into a vast, multi-level cavern—the most sacred of all magic places. Painted images were all around them, vibrant and true, crowding every surface of the rock.

It was a marvel and a miracle, a place of disbelief and wonder. Who but a Crone could form pictures in her head? Yet here, in the hidden cavern, were pictures for all to see, the holy pictures of the tribe, which ensured success in the hunt, which protected the tribe from evil, which called to the Mother of All Things and formed the firm foundation for all important magic.

The Crone awaited them, her eyes still showing the possession of the Great One within. The elders moved toward her, with their torches held high. No one spoke.

The Crone began to paint, dipping her fingers in the pots one by one and moving them across the rockface in bold, deliberate strokes. Only the Crone could create such images, as only the Crone could make pictures in her mind.

The picture took shape; and as it did so, Renka chilled. This was powerful magic indeed, the most powerful ever called up in the cavern depths. Beneath the Crone's fingers grew the image of a hunting cat, but a great cat like none the tribe had ever seen. This cat was broad of shoulder, yellow-green of eye and ferociously equipped with fangs that curled beyond its jaws like downturned mammoth tusks. The Crone called on no natural beast, but on *Saber*, the wildcat grown huge in the dream-time, who had dared defy even the Mother of All Things!

Renka heard the strangled gasp from her fellow elders as they recognized what was happening. In their war against the ogres, the Crone had decided to invoke the mystic aid of the most dangerous of all the spirit beasts.

At last it was done, the image was complete. The fire died from the Crone's eyes and she walked toward them haltingly, her hands still bright with paint. They helped her from the cavern, noticing how frequently she stumbled now, how labored her breathing had become. Behind them, as the torchlight faded, the image of the great cat Saber slowly disappeared. Yet Renka and the elders knew it still remained, lurking hidden in the darkness, watching over all they had to do.

They emerged at last beneath the anxious eyes of the waiting tribe.

"It is done," said Renka simply.

They walked forward and the Crone slumped down unconscious on the bare earth. Two young women ran to tend her, carrying her between them to the longhouse with such ease that it was obvious her old bones weighed little, like the bones of a bird.

Renka led the mass of warriors from the village then, across the plain to the great forest. As she passed beyond the circle of the now-dead ringfires, it began to rain, a chilling, steady downpour flecked with sleet.

15

Shiva and the Skull

The rhino hurtled toward her, head down, snorting like some giant boar.

Small stones were thrown up by its feet as it moved. Its stomach swung from side to side. Breath from the flaring nostrils formed plumes in the chilly morning air. It smelled of earth and dung.

Shiva ran.

A single glance told her she had wandered too far to reach the tree again, so she ran blindly, without a sense of destination. The rhino thundered after her, moving with almost unbelievable speed for a beast of its bulk. Rhinos did not hunt for hunger—they only wanted to kill.

Propelled by terror, Shiva ran faster than she had ever run before, twisting and weaving in the hope of confusing her pursuer. But still the rhino gained on her.

She reached an area of stony ground, not unlike the terrain where she had been attacked by the wolf, but there were no rocks large enough to give her shelter.

Desperation gave her a small extra burst of speed, but it stretched the distance between them by no more than the span of her hand. She looked around wildly, but there was no refuge, no tree to climb, no convenient rock, no crevice into which she could dive for safety. Still running at full speed, she jumped over a small boulder, and then the ground beneath her feet crumbled to swallow her.

In a moment of total confusion, Shiva fell, slid and rolled. She had a brief impression of thorn bushes that tore at her face and hands, then a savage pain in her side as she struck something sharp and hard. Her outstretched hands rasped off some rough surface, then she hit the bottom with such force that the breath was pounded from her body. Her consciousness whirled once, then dimmed, brightened, faded into a brown darkness.

She could not have remained unconsious for long, for when she came to, she could still hear the rhino snuffling and stamping somewhere above her head. She moved, and a small shower of grit and pebbles struck her upturned face.

She was in some sort of burrow. Shiva moved

cautiously. Her side felt as though it were on fire, and when she pulled back the skin tunic to examine herself, she found a huge, spreading blue-black bruise that oozed blood. There was blood on her hands and arms, running from a series of small scratches, and, by the feel, more blood on her face. Her left foot was twisted under her at an odd angle and seemed stiff and painful when she moved it, but after a moment that pain died.

She shifted again, half hoping to climb to her feet, when suddenly the huge head of the rhino appeared in the opening above. It was so unexpected that Shiva jumped back involuntarily and fell again, heavily, hurting her back and hip.

The rhino pushed and snorted angrily, but it could not reach her, and there was no way a beast of its size could fit through the entrance into which she had fallen. After a moment it withdrew. She waited, breathless. Soon she heard it trotting off.

Shiva sighed, relief momentarily overcoming her pains. Cautiously she crawled back up the earthen ramp, pushed past the thorn bushes and peered out. Sure enough, the thick hindquarters of the rhino were receding in the distance, tiny tail twitching angrily from side to side. She was safe. She reached up and grasped a root, hoping to pull herself from the hole, but it came away in her hand

141

so that she slid back down again, more slowly this time and without striking any rocks or thorns, but twisting as she went.

The burrow, or tunnel, or whatever it was she had fallen into, opened into a subterranean chamber, a small natural cavern rather than anything an animal had dug out. The discovery made her instantly wary. Certain she had fallen into the lair of some beast, and now that she saw the cavern, she realized suddenly it might be a very large beast indeed.

She froze into immobility, nostrils flaring as she fought to catch a scent. Something about the structure of the lair made her wonder about cave lions. Not a full pride, but a mother in cub, perhaps, looking for a place to have her young. Shiva slid a little farther down the ramp, sniffing the air. If it was a lioness, both she and her cubs were long gone. The only smells were those of earth and vegetation.

Nothing of importance ever happens by accident, remarked the voice of the Crone in her head, so vividly that Shiva started. Now why, she wondered, had she suddenly thought that?

She moved from the ramp into the cavern proper. A deep ledge, above head height, ran along the back wall of the cavern. Shiva moved forward and stepped up on a rocky outcrop so that she could see onto the ledge. As she did so her heart stopped and her breath froze in her body. Only a foot or so away from her face, staring at her with lifeless eyes, was the skull of a predator cat.

It was large, larger even than the head of a cave lion, but strangely formed, slightly flattened and broad with elongated jaws. But strangest of all were the two huge fangs that curved down from the upper jaw like tusks. They were the largest teeth she had ever seen in the head of any beast.

Behind the skull lay enormous bones, browning with age. In the heap she could recognize a broad ribcage and the curve of a massive spine. A great cat with huge, curved fangs had died here long ago and rotted, undiscovered, in its lair. But what sort of cat? What creature left behind such bones?

As she stared into the empty eye sockets of the skull, a strange thing happened. Pictures began to form unbidden in Shiva's mind. Since early childhood she had played with pictures in her head, but nothing like this. They came so vividly, so clearly, she felt she could almost step into them. . . .

She was looking across a broad sweep of tundra so chilled that nothing grew save a few stunted plants and patches of some hardy moss. The earth

143

beneath her feet was frozen almost to the consistency of rock, and she could feel the chill winds from the north reach out to pluck her heavy clothing and steal the small heat imprisoned in her shivering body.

To the north and northwest she could see what at first appeared to be a range of mountains, shrouded in perpetual mist. But then the mist parted and she knew she was looking at a cliff of ice that towered so high she could not see its upper surface. Shiva knew the ice cliff was moving, inching forward relentlessly with such slow force that it ground down any rocks before it as if they were dried clay.

The mists closed in again, white and opaque; and for the first time in her young life Shiva knew she had been granted a vision of something sung of in the ballad histories of the tribe—the chill, dreadful, barren kingdom of Mamar, God of Ice.

But breathtaking as was the vision of the ice cliff, Shiva found her whole attention drawn to something else. Padding across the tundra, head high and proud, was a gigantic cat. The pictures in her mind were now so vivid it might have stood in front of her. The thick coat was yellow-white, like the fur of the northern bears. The paws were broad like the paws of a cave lion, but flatter, as

144

if the creature often walked in snow. There was heavy muscling at the shoulders, the heaviest she had seen in any cat. The body might have been that of a snow leopard grown huge, but the head was the head of a tiger. And from the jaws curved two gigantic fangs, like mammoth tusks turned downward. As far as she could judge, the creature stood a little higher than her head.

Shiva released a single, explosive breath. Only one beast ever looked like that. She was watching Saber, the wildcat grown beyond his natural size, banished forever from the dreamtime and wandering the edges of Mamar's icy kingdom.

Shiva blinked and the vision faded. She stared inward, watching the vision recede. It had come, from far away and long ago. But it was linked with the reality before her. Had Saber wandered south to hunt? Or had Mamar's kingdom extended to this land in those distant days? She did not know, but of one thing she was certain: The bones before her were the bones of Saber.

She reached forward like one in a trance and touched a fang. Saber! Beneath her hand was the tooth of a creature from the dreamtime!

Here was mighty magic indeed, perhaps the greatest magic the tribe had ever known. Here lay the bones of the only beast to defy the Mother. With such bones the Crone might work a miracle.

Hard on the thought came another. With such bones might she not return to the tribe?

The idea caught her with growing excitement. She had never wanted to leave, only to release the little ogre. Until now, there had seemed no turning back. But now . . . How could they turn her away? How could they turn away one so favored by the Mother that she had discovered the grave of Saber?

The thought grew large and possessed her entirely. She would mark the spot and return to the camp. They would be angry, of course, because she had freed the little ogre. But then she would tell them about her find. Her name would be added to the histories. She would be welcome in the tribe forever.

She started excitedly back up the ramp, but stopped as a new thought struck her. What if they did not believe?

Shiva half ran, half slid back down the ramp, crossed the cave and climbed up on the ledge. She would take one of the bones. She would show it to the elders and the Crone, and they would know she told the truth.

Which bone? All were large, all were impressive, yet she hesitated. For a long moment Shiva sat, excited, fearful, tense and undecided. Then, in a single impulsive movement she seized the skull and jumped down from the ledge.

It was cumbersome and heavy, so heavy that she staggered a little under its weight, but her high excitement helped her get it up the ramp. She emerged from the hole to discover that the sky had clouded over and it had begun to rain. She looked around for the little ogre, anxious to tell someone of her find, even someone who would not understand. But the little ogre was nowhere to be seen.

Shiva's excitement died at once. She had almost forgotten the little ogre, forgotten the reality of her situation. He had saved her life and when she had set him free, he would not leave without her. Would not, or could not . . .

In her deepest heart, Shiva knew something very special about the little ogre. He was ugly, he was stubborn, he was strong, but beyond all this and more importantly, he was still a little boy. He could not skin a wolf. He could not avoid the hunters who had captured him.

And he could not find his own way home!

The real reason why he stayed so close to her was that he needed her.

Where was he now? Ogres, she knew, lived in the deep forest, in caves so dark that humans could not find their way within them. This was the reason—one reason—why the forest was avoided. Perhaps the little ogre had gone back there. . . .

Shiva sighed. How could she find his cave when she had never even stepped within the forest in her life?

Had he gone alone to the forest? Had he thought her dead now, trampled by the rhino? Was he trying to find his way home alone?

She looked down at Saber's skull, tilted to one side on the ground. It would be better if she went back quickly. She would show them the skull and they would welcome her. No one would even mention she had freed the little ogre . . . who was trying to find his way home alone.

Stupid boy! But she owed him nothing now. She had freed him from the cage. She had even made sure he got away safely from the camp. She had showed him how to evade the hunters by walking in a stream. They were even now. She owed him nothing. Nothing.

Alone. In the forest alone.

He was an ogre, for goodness' sake. He lived in the forest! He knew the forest far better than she did. She had never even been inside the forest. Besides, she owed him nothing.

In her mind, his hand reached out to her.

She owed him nothing. She would have escaped from the stupid wolf the same way she had escaped from the rhino. She owed him nothing. And besides, it would be absolutely senseless for her to try to find him in the forest.

The rain was heavier now and chill with sleet, but at least it would wash the caked blood from her face and hands. Shiva sighed again. Half dragging Saber's massive skull, she set off toward the forest.

16
Hiram's Trial

"We shall hold a trial!" Thag proclaimed. "We shall hold it in the hall of judgment. I shall sit on the Rock of Judgment. We shall hold our trial before the men of the clan, and the women will stay away." He looked pointedly at Hana, who ignored him.

Thag drew a deep breath. "We shall hold the trial *now*!" He turned and loped toward the caves. . . .

Hiram shivered. He felt sick and very, very frightened. The rank stench of ogre oozed like birch sap through his nose and down his throat. Distant ogres had been terrifying enough, but ogres close up had a horror unmatched by anything he had ever known. He would rather sleep with a pride of cave lions than come close to a single ogre. But he was close now, captured in the night, destined to be eaten, and there was nothing he could do about it.

He took a deep, shuddering breath in an attempt to bring his emotions under control. The ogres had dragged him, screaming, through the dark forest, and now, in the first light of dawn, he was in a clearing underneath some cavern-riddled cliff, surrounded by ogres.

He thought of chieftain Renka's plan for a raid on the forest and shivered again. A hunting party here would be torn apart and eaten within minutes. No one in the tribe had any real idea how horrible the ogres really were, how large, how strong, how fierce, how *many*.

One of the brutes shoved its face close to his and growled something that might have been an order. Could ogres speak? Did they have a language as humans did? The barbarous, guttural sounds that issued from their throats were more like the grunts and coughs of animals, but he imagined they could understand each other at some very primitive level.

The creature growled at him again, then, when he did not respond, seized him by the upper arm.

He was being dragged toward the caves! Hiram twisted, struggled and struck out, but he might as well have been beating his fists against solid rock.

The ogre ignored him. He was dragged across the clearing. In a moment the gloom of the cave mouth closed around him.

"Why," Hana asked, "do you want to hold a trial?"

"They took my son," Thag growled. "They must be punished."

"They?" Hana asked. *"They*? Do you put *them* on trial? Do you punish *them*? How can trying this one Weakling Stranger punish *them*?" Was there ever anyone so stupid as this man of hers? He had taken one of the Strangers and the whole accursed tribe would soon come searching for him. That was their way. Had he even posted guards? Would the clan be given warning before the Strangers came to kill them?

"He stands trial in place of his tribe," Thag explained. He glowered at her. "You can't come— you're a woman." He placed one huge hand on her chest, but withdrew it when she tried to bite him.

"Why not wait?" Hana asked furiously. "Why not wait a little while and then you can put the whole Weakling Stranger tribe on trial!"

"What?" muttered Thag. "What?" He frowned, not understanding.

"They will follow him here—here to the forest.

They will follow him with their spears and their clubs, and they will kill the people of the clan as they have always killed the people of the clan!"

"How will they follow him?" Thag demanded. "They do not know the forest trails."

"Did you cover your trail?"

"No, we—"

"Did you walk in water to hide your scent?"

Thag shuddered. "No, but—"

"Then how will they not follow you, Thag? How will they not? Have you posted guards?"

"I shall post guards!" Thag roared abruptly. He turned and struck a man named Khar, who happened to be standing near him. "I, Thag, shall post guards so that the Weakling Strangers will not creep up on us. I shall post guards *on the edge of the forest!*"

"Let's hope you're not too late," Hana muttered.

There was some sort of fight going on between the big, ugly male ogre and the small white-haired female, Hiram noticed. The male was a monster, even in this monstrous clan. But he seemed nervous of the female and once, when he reached out to touch her, she snapped at him with the ferocity of a wildcat. Now the big brute was running about, pushing and shoving his fellow males.

The male holding Hiram dragged him along a

narrow passage and into a huge cavern lit by torches, some held by members of the clan, others stuck in grooves and cracks according to no apparent plan. Large though the cavern was, the combined stench of ogre bodies and smoke was almost overpowering. Hiram coughed, then gagged, but somehow managed to prevent himself from becoming sick. Was this where they would kill him?

The big male ogre who had fought with the white-haired female burst through the throng, scattering those around him, and climbed up on a flat-topped rock. He turned to face the rest, growled, twitched, scratched himself and squatted.

"Let the trial begin!" Thag proclaimed from his position on the Rock of Judgment. "I, Thag, will be the Judge." He glared around him, daring intervention. If there was going to be a challenge to his authority, it would most likely come now, since if he lost a fight in the judgment hall, he would immediately cease to be leader of the clan.

But for once there was no challenge. Even Shil seemed withdrawn and subdued.

Thag rocked back on his heels, scarcely noticing as Hagar took his traditional place on his right side and a little to the rear. "We meet to try the Weakling Stranger!" Thag roared, sweeping his arm in a dramatic arc. To his delight, Mabango pushed the

154

Stranger to the fore: beautifully timed. Thag pushed his lips outward, then withdrew them to reveal his teeth. "We will judge the Weakling Stranger *who stole my son*!"

There was a roar of deep approval from the clan.

"How do you know?" asked a familiar voice sharply when the noise eventually died down.

If Hiram had not known better, he might have thought it was some sort of religious ceremony. Then again, perhaps it was. Crude and primitive though they were, the ogres were not, perhaps, totally lacking feelings. Gloom settled over him like a cloud. The ceremony—if it was a ceremony— would be one of sacrifice.

Thag looked down from the Judgment Seat. Hana was not supposed to be here. He had told her. He had told her *only the men*! He had told her and told her and told her and still she would not listen!

"How do I know what?" Thag roared.

"How do you know this was the one who stole our son?" Hana asked.

Thag blinked and began to rock back and forth on his heels. He frowned. Eventually he shouted, "Is he not a Weakling Stranger?"

There were growls of approval from the assembled men. Men understood these things. Men

155

understood law and justice. Men knew he was the strongest of the clan.

"Would you try Mabango because Shil stole Heft's meat?" Hana asked him bluntly.

Thag frowned. Meat? Why was she talking about meat? Then, quite suddenly, he saw what she was getting at. "That is different!" he roared. He considered ordering the men to drag her out, but did not dare.

"How is it different?" Hana shouted back. "And why do you waste time on this stupid trial when you still have not found our son!"

An icy clutch of fear rose up to grip Thag's heart. He did not like to think too much of Doban. The boy was no longer at the Strangers' camp. He had escaped from the cage, for even though he was still a child, he was strong, as his father was strong. He had escaped without help, on his own, using his strength to tear apart the wicker cage. He had run bravely into the night. They had not found him, but Heft the Hunter tracked him even now. He would be found soon. No living thing could escape Heft the Hunter. He would be found soon.

But he was not found yet, and there were many dangers in the night and many dangers in the day. Until Heft found him and brought him back, Thag did not like to think of Doban, for thoughts of Doban ate pieces from his heart.

"Heft is bringing Doban back!" he screamed.

"Has Heft found him?" Hana screamed back. "Does *anybody* know where Doban is?"

Thag launched himself from the Judgment Seat. He cut a path through the assembled crowd, flinging men aside in all directions. He stamped his feet and roared wordlessly, great fists pounding on the rocks.

Hiram jerked away, heart pounding. The largest male had gone berserk, hurling himself through the cavern like a demon. There was pandemonium as the remaining ogres fought to get out of his way, half climbing over one another in panic. The creature holding Hiram's arm slackened his grip and Hiram seized his chance. He twisted, ducked and ran, weaving between the milling ogre bodies, terror lending speed to his legs.

"Now look what you've done!" Thag howled accusingly at Hana.

Hiram ran. He ran faster than he had ever run before, faster than any hunter of the tribe. He leaped rocks and dodged descending outcrops, brushed aside the hairy arms that sought to seize him. A monster loomed in front of him and Hiram, following some instinct that ran deeper than courage, deeper than fear, lowered his head and ran full speed to butt it in the stomach. The monster sat down with a whoosh of exploding breath.

Hiram vaulted over it and ran full tilt for the entrance of the cave.

"After him!" screamed Thag. "Catch him! Don't let him escape!"

Four ogres rushed toward him, collided into one another, and fell down in an ungainly heap. Hiram avoided them easily and reached the narrow passageway that led out of the cavern.

"He has got away!" Thag roared at Hana. "You have let him get away!" He fell on his knees and began to pound the rock floor with both fists.

Hagar came to kneel beside him. "He may still be recaptured, Mighty Chieftain," he whispered.

Thag stopped pounding. "He may?"

"He is a Weakling Stranger," Hagar whispered. "Even if he finds his way out of the caverns, he will not find his way out of the forest. We will track him easily."

The passageway out of the cavern branched and joined with others to create a confusing maze. But Hiram had a hunter's instinct and did not waver for an instant. Behind him he could hear the clamor of pursuit, but that did not trouble him. He knew that if he reached the open, he could outrun any ogre who had ever lived—especially in his present state of terror.

What did trouble him—and troubled him to a

degree that tripled his terror—was the possibility of meeting up with another ogre in the front.

But all the ogres, it seemed, were in the cavern behind him. Or if not, they were somewhere else far distant in the caves. He met no one, no one at all. He ran, heart bursting, until he reached the first cavern, the cavern entrance. He saw the new light of day and it had never looked so wonderful.

Hiram still ran. He ran from the entrance and ran across the clearing, and knowing he would soon escape, he ran with joy.

And as he ran, he saw a warrior step into the clearing.

He almost stopped, but his momentum kept him going. Another warrior emerged from the forest, then another and another. He saw Renka, the chief, and his friends from the hunt. He saw the blood-red faces of the warrior women and the death-white faces of the warrior men. He saw the spears and the clubs and the sticks and the stones, and he knew that everything was going to be all right. He would not be killed. Everything was going to be all right, all right, all right. . . .

Behind him, the fastest of the ogre clan swarmed from the cavern entrance.

In the Dark Forest

There was something stalking her.

Rain rustled incessantly on the new-leaf canopy in the upper terraces of the forest so that all other sounds were muffled. Shiva's nostrils were filled with the scents of resins, damp earth, moss and vegetation. Nonetheless, some sixth sense told her she was being stalked as surely as if she could see the creature with her eyes. Her neck hairs prickled and there was a mild but definite sensation of pressure in her back. The feeling of menace was strong, stronger even than the time she had been stalked by the wolf.

She did not like the forest. From the moment she had entered, she felt uncomfortable and chill with a coldness that had nothing to do with a biting wind that moaned and whispered through the trees. It was a place of gloom, of murmurs, of strange noises and stranger smells. And to someone accustomed to the landmarks of an open world, it had a sameness that was utterly confusing. Luckily she had found a narrow trail and stuck to it. Without that she would have been entirely lost.

But with it she was going nowhere.

She had seen no signs whatsoever of the little ogre, no signs of anything at all except trees. How could she find him in a place so vast?

The little ogre might have followed this path, or might not—she did not know. She followed it doggedly, with all the stubborn patience of one who does not know what else to do. Her arms ached from the weight of Saber's skull.

Was that a sound? The forest was full of sounds, a chatter of noises that blended with the backdrop of the hissing rain, but was that a special, sinister sound?

Shiva turned abruptly. There was nothing on the trail behind her.

She forced herself to relax. This was silly, too silly to be endured. She had entered the forest only minutes before and already she was starting like a frightened rabbit at every little unfamiliar noise. But the trouble was *every* noise was unfamiliar. She was of the tribe and those of the tribe did not enter the forest.

She pushed forward, locked in an inner dialogue.

Should she go back? She had lost the little ogre. She knew that now.

She glanced around her. She had no hope of finding him in this huge forest. For all she knew, he might not even be here. He might be miles away across the open plain. He might be hidden in some cave. He might even have found his own way home, wherever home might be. He might be anywhere. She would never find him.

But at least she had tried. She had released him from the cage, taken him from the camp and tried to find him when she lost him. What more could she do? She had the great skull now, the magic skull of the wildcat grown huge. It was all she needed.

That was a sound!

Shiva swung around again and this time saw—or thought she saw—a movement in the undergrowth a distance behind and to the right. Without the slightest hesitation, she plunged left, seized by an instinct that spurred action without argument.

Climb a tree, whispered the imaginary figure of her mother in her ear. But the branches of the trees here were high above her head. She might still climb, but not easily and not quickly. Besides, there was the skull.

Leave the skull, her mother said.

162

But Shiva could not leave the skull.

Without the skull they might never let her back into the tribe after what she had done. Without the skull there was nothing to apply against her crime in releasing the little ogre.

And besides, the skull was not merely magic, but *her* magic. *She* had fallen into Saber's lair. *She* had found the bones. *She* had recognized their worth. *She* had carried off the skull.

Nothing of importance ever happens by accident, murmured the voice of the Crone in her mind. In a special way she did not understand, but clearly felt, the skull was bound to her.

She blundered on, desperately searching for a tree with branches low enough to climb.

Her arms and hands began to bleed again as she burst through a clump of thorny bushes, which ripped at her like frightened cats. She did not know where she was going, only that she must run.

She ran between trees and around bushes and once leaped a narrow, shallow stream. At length she broke through into a hollow. Two trees had fallen to form bridges, giants made strange now, their branches stretching up instead of out, like pleading arms.

Several more trees leaned at a drunken angle where the ground had subsided. Three were climbable. She picked that nearest and ran up the inclining trunk, easily able to carry the skull.

Luck climbed with her, for she discovered a platform of woven branches, the nest of some tree dweller now moved on, and left the skull there, wedged for safety, before climbing farther. The tree leaned against another more upright and this she climbed as well until, shaking with tension and exhaustion, she felt herself safe.

She set her back against the trunk, squatted on a thick branch, stared down and waited.

Nothing came.

Shiva waited, sniffing the air and listening. Overhead the rain dripped through the canopy, but she was already too wet to care.

Still nothing. Had she been mistaken? For someone unaccustomed to the forest, the smallest noise might turn, in her imagination, into monsters. She thought of going down.

Wait, her mother said.

Shiva waited. As she waited, her mind came to a decision. When the way was clear, she would go back to the trail and leave the forest. She would return with the skull of Saber to her tribe. She had done all she could do for the little ogre who had saved her life. Now it was time to go home.

She waited. Still nothing came, no wolf, no bear, no cat. She would go home. She was frightened of the forest and had done all she could for her little friend. She would take the skull of Saber and go back to her tribe.

Her gaze crossed the hollow one more time. No creature stirred. Without conscious decision, she started down the tree.

Wait, the spirit of her mother said again.

Everybody talked of spirits—the spirits of the stream, the spirits of the wind, the spirits of the tree, the spirits of the ancestors—but few claimed actually to see them. Except for the Crone, who could make pictures in her head.

As Shiva could make pictures in her head.

She blinked, thoughtfully. There was a difference between *making* pictures and what happened when she played imaginary games. She did not *imagine* a wobble running through the bushes—it did that of its own accord.

Could these be *spirits?*

She wished, desperately, that there were someone she could talk to who could also make pictures in the head. Perhaps the Crone, except that like so many others of the tribe, Shiva was very frightened of the Crone. She still shivered at the memory of their meeting in the Ring of Stones. The Crone had been kindly enough then, even gentle, but still she frightened Shiva.

Hiram? She liked Hiram and was certain he

could make pictures in his head. But she had never spoken to him about it directly, never even admitted her own talent. To do so might make her vulnerable, although she did not quite know how. It was best to keep her secrets to herself, tell no one, reveal herself to no one.

Were they spirits? Was she sister to some elemental creatures?

The thought excited her almost as much as finding Saber's lair. Could she actually see *spirits*? Was this what people meant when they talked about the Crone's powers? Was this what she did?

Out of nowhere, Shiva wondered what it would be like to be a Crone. Not all Crones were as ancient as the Crone of her tribe, but all were full of wisdom and respected. Might she become a Crone one day?

The thought struck her suddenly as funny, and she giggled in a way she had not done for years. Then she sobered. Was it really so ridiculous? The Crone lived and the Crone died and another Crone took her place. The present Crone was very old, had been with the tribe for many, many years. One day she must be gathered to the Mother, as all things were gathered to the Mother. Then who would be Crone?

Shiva knew little of how Crones were made. She had heard it said, vaguely, that each Crone must train a new Crone to take her place when she died. But the Crone of the tribe trained no one, of that she was sure. Some said she had not yet found any woman suitable. But she must begin to train a woman soon, for she was very, very old.

Where would the Crone find someone suitable to train? Why had they met in the Ring of Stones?

Nothing—nothing of importance—ever happens by accident.

Shiva reached the nest of woven branches and took up the skull again, tugging to free one curled tooth that had become caught among the twigs. It felt strangely warm to the touch, as if a part of her had reached beyond the bone to touch the living beast itself.

She carried the skull carefully to the forest floor, as one might carry a sacred object—which, she supposed, it was, since it had belonged to a creature of the dreamtime. She balanced it on the sloping trunk, slid down to the forest floor, then turned to retrieve it. As she did so, a monstrous shape rose up from the undergrowth to embrace her.

Shiva dropped the skull and screamed. A potent scent was in her nostrils now, the same scent she had smelled from the ogre boy who had saved her from the wolf. She saw fangs and matted hair, a body where the muscles intertwined like tree roots, a face from a nightmare on a massive, deformed head. She pounded at the creature with her fists in a spasm of wild panic.

She was caught by an ogre.

The thing released her. She tried to run, but there was nowhere to flee to. The tree trunk was at her back, dense bushes to her left, while the monster faced her, arms outstretched, like one herding game. Shiva's heart pounded with such force, she thought it must burst from her chest. Could she climb the tree again? But ogres could climb trees easily, as easily as humans—even more so. There would be no escape that way.

She dodged to one side, but the monster moved to block her. It was remarkably light on its feet and swift for something of its bulk. She dodged again, but still it blocked her. What could she do? What could she do? Desperately she looked around, her eyes dark like those of a frightened bird.

Then, behind the brute, she saw another, smaller form. He shuffled toward her in that familiar crouching gait and pushed past the larger ogre with a gesture almost of impatience. He stopped less than a yard away from her, half squatted and gazed at her with those huge, brown, liquid eyes. His lips writhed and a series of guttural sounds emerged.

Shiva remained immobile, staring at him, thunderstruck. It was her little ogre! It was her little ogre back with his own kind! She glanced at the beast beyond, a creature of such supreme ugliness that she shivered involuntarily even to look at it. Was this the little ogre's father?

The little ogre reached out and tugged at her clothing. He repeated the guttural sounds, the first noise she had ever heard him make. His eyes locked on hers.

Suddenly she realized he was speaking. Nothing else made sense. The little ogre was *speaking* to her. The sounds reached her as a garble: *sa eftuntrr . . . iva sa eftuntrr.*

Shiva shook her head. He was speaking his own tongue. Ogres had a language! They could talk together! But astonishing though that was, it did not help her understand him. She shook her head again, wondering how to tell him she did not know what he was saying.

"Sa eftuntrr iva! Sa eftuntrr!" He turned and looked at the towering beast behind him. *"Iva, sa eftuntrr!"* The larger ogre stared back, saying nothing. He had brown eyes like the boy, so dark they were almost black.

"Little ogre," Shiva whispered, "I know you are talking to me, but I do not understand you." There was something in the moment that took away her fear, although nervousness remained when she looked at the great beast behind him.

The little ogre was growing excitable, or possibly impatient. *"Iva, sa eftuntrr!"* he shouted, tugging at her clothes. He jumped up and down and once, in frustration, struck the trunk of the tree with the back of his hand. *"Iva, sa eftuntrr! Iva, sa eftuntrr!"*

Then suddenly, as if a branch had snapped inside her head, she knew he was not speaking his own language, but hers. It was incredible, but it was true. He spoke it badly, with an accent so barbarous it might well have been a foreign tongue. But he spoke it—she was sure.

She concentrated hard. *Sa eftuntrr . . . iva sa eftuntrr.* And again: *eftuntrr . . . iva sa eftuntrr.* There was a strange familiarity about the—

She had it! She had it!

The little ogre looked at her. "Shiva," he said, pointing at the nightmare standing behind him, "this is Heft the Hunter."

18
Human Tribe Meets Ogre Clan

She felt as a bird might feel, flying low through the forest branches, watching movement as the trees whipped past her, one after one, and feeling . . . safe. For the first time in her life, as long as she could remember, feeling totally protected from any creature who would make her prey.

She was sitting on the big ogre's shoulders, the skull of Saber cradled in her arms, clinging to him with her knees while he ran through the forest like a great cat, following trails she could not see, neither stopping nor pausing nor even slowing. Beside him, trotting comfortably in the same strange, crouched loping gait, face expressionless, was her little ogre. His name was *Doban*.

And the monster between her knees was Heft the Hunter. Except he did not seem a monster now.

His body was warm, the massive muscles firm and strong. The ogre scent that rose from him was musty, but not at all unpleasant. It reminded her of the scents of the forest, a resin smell with hints of deep, safe caves. Even the heavy body hair, which had seemed so frightening, felt softer than she had expected, like fur.

The sensation of movement was exhilarating. Shiva flung back her head and drank in the forest air, she felt more alive than she had ever felt before, and there was an excitement in her that danced and sparkled like sunlight on a swiftly moving stream. She did not quite know where they were going, but she thought they might be going to the ogre clan.

How strange it was she felt no fear. In her mind, she tried to recall ogre stories she had heard as a child. But the stories had lost their power. She knew the names of ogres now—Doban and Heft the Hunter—and ogres did not frighten her.

She wished Doban could talk a little better. He knew only a few words and even those she had great difficulty making out. It was as if his jaw and tongue and throat were the wrong shape for making words, so that everything emerged rolling, like a pebble down a rock slope. All the same, it was a miracle he could make any words at all, for he must have learned them in the short time he had been captured by the tribe.

Which meant, the sudden thought occurred to her, he must be a great deal more clever than she had imagined.

She glanced across and down at him, loping easily alongside Heft the Hunter, and such warmth welled up from her stomach that she smiled. Although it was strange to her, she knew the emotion for what it was. Doban, the little ogre, was her friend.

Bouncing on the broad, warm back of Heft the Hunter, a new thought occurred to Shiva. If Doban found such difficulty with her language, perhaps she could learn his. She knew the ogres talked to one another as easily as humans did, a stream of words and gestures that reminded her of some deep, raucous birdsong. Perhaps she could learn the words and use them. What times they would have together then! He could show her the deep caves and the ways of his people. They could walk together in the forest and she would not be afraid. There were so many, many things that they might learn from one another. He might even be able to make pictures in his mind, although she doubted that.

Heft stopped and gestured so that Shiva slid

down from his shoulders. He seemed to be listening. Shiva sniffed the air, but could pick up no unusual scents; and her ears told her nothing. Doban too seemed ill at ease, glancing around him with sudden caution. They began to move forward together, all three, slowly. Suddenly Shiva heard it. Voices! And the voices of her tribe! Too far away to make out words, but definite.

"It's—" she began excitedly. But the little ogre tugged her arm to silence her.

They moved forward again at a slow, cautious trot and suddenly the forest thinned. Gently Heft pushed apart two bushes and she was looking into a broad clearing, bounded to her left by the upward sweep of a sheer rock face. As she did so, a great many things began to happen.

A figure emerged from a cave in the rock face, running. It took her a surprised instant to realize it was Hiram.

At the far side, distant from him, the chieftain Renka stepped into the clearing, followed almost at once by two warriors whose left hands clutched flint-tipped spears. The face of one warrior was painted blood red with ocher pigment. The other, a man, was smeared with gray-white clay so that she could not recognize him. But she knew what it meant. These were the colors of blood and bone. These were the colors of war.

Ogres swarmed from the cave mouth behind Hiram. One of them was even bigger than Heft the Hunter.

Hiram flung himself on his knees before his chieftain. "Thank you," he gasped. "Oh, thank you, Lady Renka!" He clutched at the bindings of her leggings. "Thank you," he said. "Thank you. Thank you. Thank you."

"Get up, you fool," said Renka sourly. Behind him, on the far side of the clearing, she could see the ogres. They poured from the caverns in an un-ending stream, spreading like spilled blood.

Spilled blood . . .

There were so many of them. Renka had not believed there could be so many ogres in the world. Not one ogre had been seen by any of the tribe for close on two generations. Even Hiram claimed to have seen no more than three. But here, by the forest cliff, the ogres were as many as sand grains on the shore.

She looked up. The cliff face was peppered with caves and there were ogre faces peering from each one. Even as she watched, more ogres began to climb down the sheer rock.

If they attacked, there would be much spilled blood.

The tribe would win the battle—of that Renka had no doubt. Not one of the monsters spreading out before her carried a single spear. Few seemed to be carrying weapons of any sort. But they were huge and they were strong and they were agile and they were legion. Many of the tribe would never see tomorrow's dawn. Did the winning of the battle make up for that?

"They were going to eat me, Lady Renka," Hiram said, pushing himself to his feet. "They took me into the caves and growled at me and talked among themselves about how to eat me." His eyes were shining as he babbled with relief.

He was safe now, Renka thought—at least as safe as any of them. He was one reason for this war and he was safe. But the orphan Shiva was still prisoner.

She supposed.

Renka felt more nervous, ill at ease, confused than at any time since she had become the chief. "Do you know the girl Shiva? Do the ogres have her?" It was possible—just possible—that the ogres did not. And if they did not, was there any reason for this war? Was there any reason for good women and their men to die? Once she might have attacked the ogres merely because of what they were. But not now. Not when it would cost so much in blood. So many of them, yet no ogre had harmed any from the tribes in two generations.

Best it should remain so, each going separate ways.

Hiram shook his head. "I don't know. I did not see her."

He saw Lightning Birds and sacred groves and ogre packs outside the forest, but he never saw what it was useful to see! Where was Shiva? Where was the girl?

A cold thought came to Renka. Was one young orphan worth a war? Her parents were dead. The girl herself seemed capable enough, but there was nothing in her that was special, nothing of more than average value to the tribe. Hiram was a hunter and a good one for all his fancies. His mother Sheena was the Keeper of the Sacred Drums. He had his worth.

But Hiram was safe now. Only Shiva remained. Could the life of one young orphan justify a war?

Renka was torn. As chieftain of the tribe she had no mate, no children of her own. Yet, in a way, the children of the tribe were all her children. How could she leave one to the mercy of the ogres?

How could she lead many to be slaughtered by the ogres? her heart asked her in return.

She felt the pressure of bodies around her as more and more of her warriors emerged into the forest clearing. Before her, the stream of ogres from the caves had ceased and the heaving mass of the monsters had become very still. As she watched, an exceptionally large and ugly ogre pushed his way to the front.

"I am Thag!" roared Thag across the clearing in the ancient challenge to these Weakling Strangers who had entered his domain intent on threatening his people. "I am strong! I am the strongest of the clan!" He curled one huge hand into a fist and struck his chest. "Go home to your village, Strangers. Go home *now*, or else Thag will *drive* you home."

None moved. It was as if they had not heard him.

"I am strong!" roared Thag again. He leaped fiercely in the air, dropped into a squat and pounded on the ground before him with both fists as if it were a drum. Then he stood up, straightening to his full height so that he towered above the Strangers, towered even higher than the remainder of his clan.

"I am strong!" screamed Thag. "I hurl your leader to the ground!" He made a darting run forward to frighten them and stopped.

Behind Renka, a white-faced warrior unloosed a sling. The stone hurled toward Thag with deadly force.

"No!" Hana screamed. She stepped before her

178

mate and the stone took her on the temple above her right eye.

"No!" shrieked Doban. He broke from Shiva's side and ran into the clearing as his mother fell.

Thag stared down at the crumpled body of his tiny mate and felt pain in his heart. He dropped to his knees and caught her in his arms. A wail of anguish, like the sorrows of a whole world, erupted from his throat.

Behind Renka, another warrior drew back his spear.

"No!" howled Shiva, and burst into the clearing as the little ogre leaped before the trembling spear.

The effect was like a sudden thunderclap. The warrior with the spear froze into immobility, eyes wide.

"Saber!" whispered Renka, half to herself, in wonder. She stared at the great skull still clutched in Shiva's hands and stared beyond it in her mind to the image on the hidden cavern wall. The Crone had known all this would come to pass! The Crone had known!

"Saber!" she whispered again, and this time the word was taken up by those around her.

"Saber . . ." muttered a warrior woman.

"Saber!" screamed a warrior man.

"Saber . . . Saber . . . Saber . . ." the word went

through the tribe like ripples on the surface of the sea. "Saber . . . The girl has brought us Saber. . . ."

What did it mean? What did it mean? The magic was there for all to see, but what did it mean?

Those nearest Renka fell back a single pace.

"Leave them alone!" screamed Shiva. "They are my friends!"

They understood. The orphan girl who carried the great magic had spoken clearly. Even before the sign from chieftain Renka, they began to move back, out of the clearing.

Thag saw the first retreating steps and felt his sorrow turn to wildest rage. Gently he laid aside the body of his mate and raised himself to his full height, his lips drawn back so that his great teeth were revealed.

"Thag will kill!" he roared. "Thag will kill the Weakling Strangers who have slain his mate!" He raised his arms above his head in preparation for the charge.

"Thag will be quiet and behave himself!" snapped a familar voice close by his feet. "Are you so stupid that you can't see they're leaving?"

"Hana . . . ?" Thag whispered, looking down.

She climbed a little unsteadily to her feet. The wound on her forehead oozed blood onto the prominent brow ridge, but not much.

"Hana!" Thag breathed again and wrapped his huge arms around her.

She allowed herself to be drawn close. "See," she said close by his ear. "See, Doban has returned."

They looked across at their son. His face showed trust and happiness. He was standing crouched, hand linked to hand with a young Stranger girl.

Epilogue

If you'd bought the first edition of this book, the Epilogue you're now reading would have started out:

Much of this story is true.

There really were ogres in Europe around 30, 000 years ago. They were squat, hairy creatures, heavy muscled, heavy jawed and with the same prominent brow ridge as Thag and his companions. Today we call them Neanderthals. We know quite a lot about the way they looked from the bones they left behind, but some things—such as their posture and the way they moved—are still largely guesswork.

I still believe a lot of the foregoing story is true. I also still believe there really were ogres in prehistory. Every human culture has myths and legends about great strong ugly creatures, terrifying to look at, who were enemies of humanity—and those legends had to start somewhere.

But it may not have been accurate to call the ogres Neanderthals.

Let's not get it wrong twice. There definitely were Neanderthals in Shiva's day. They were human, but not the same sort of humans we are: *Homo sapiens neanderthalensis*, not *Homo sapiens sapiens*, as the scientists would say. They had more powerful jaws and more powerful muscles and a differently shaped head. You'd be wary if you met one in the dark. They looked ugly and threatening. That's why I thought they might be good candidates for ogres.

But when I told you about Doban, Hana, and the others of the ogre Clan, I described hairy creatures who walked bent over, shuffled on flat feet, snapped and growled as much as talked, and climbed like monkeys.

The trouble with all that is the Neanderthals *didn't* walk bent over and didn't shuffle on flat feet. We once thought they did, soon after the first Neanderthal fossil bones were found in 1856 by quarrymen in a cave in the Neander Valley, near Düsseldorf, in Germany. A British biologist named Thomas Henry Huxley emphasized the more primitive aspects of the fossils and suggested they formed a link between modern humans and the apes. His view was that Neanderthals were primitive creatures, bent-kneed, half-witted, and subhuman.

But Huxley's report came out in 1863. Since then a lot of scientists have changed their minds. They now believe the only reason any Neanderthal walked bent over was arthritis, and a healthy Neanderthal was as upright as young Hiram in this book. And far from being half-witted, Neanderthals had brains as big as yours or mine. (Differently developed, but just as big.)

They were also skillful. Throughout Europe, the Middle East, and North Africa, stone tools have been discovered in association with Neanderthal remains. These include scrapers, knives, chisels, points, cleavers, and blades, all of which exhibit superior workmanship. Whatever else Neanderthals might have been, they were not primitive subhumans; they were not ogres.

This leaves us with the problem of where the ogre legends started. With *Homo sapiens neanderthalensis* out of the running, I'm beginning to wonder if a more suitable candidate altogether might not be *Gigantopithecus*.

The "pithecus" in the name gives you the clue that we're not talking about something human—*Gigantopithecus* was a breed of ape. But there are peculiarities about his teeth that may nudge him closer to humanity. Although scientists don't much like the term, you might say he was a sort of ape-man.

He was a very *big* ape-man, somewhere about the size and strength of a gorilla, but with even larger teeth. And like the gorilla, he may have been an essentially gentle creature who relied on his immense size, strength, and threatening manner to keep other animals in line. If you think that sounds a bit like Thag, I'd agree with you.

We know for certain *Gigantopithecus* lived in Asia, because we've found his fossil bones there. We don't know for certain if he lived in Europe or America or anywhere else, but I suspect he may have, for reasons I'll go into in a moment. He was still roaming around China as recently as 500,000 years ago. In geological time, that isn't wildly removed from the era, 125,000 years ago, when we have our first evidence of Neanderthals.

Could *Gigantopithecus* have survived long enough to become Shiva's secret friend? Most scientists would say no. As far as they are concerned, *Gigantopithecus* became extinct a half a million years ago.

But there are a few—just a few—who think *Gigantopithecus* lingered on in a few remote corners of the world . . . even to the present day. He is seen occasionally in the Himalayas, where the natives call him the *yeti* or "abominable snowman." He is seen occasionally in the forests of northwest America, where he gets the name *sasquatch,* or "bigfoot."

Those who have seen the yeti or the sasquatch say he is big and ugly and fearsome, but that he will only harm humans if they corner him and spends most of his time hiding himself away in remote places. He has hidden so successfully for so long that most humans don't believe he exists at all.

And if that doesn't sound like Thag and his Clan, I don't know what does.

If *Gigantopithicus* really roamed the forests of the Ice Age, he was not the only weird creature about. Other strange beasts included the hippo Hiram saw, the woolly rhino that chased Shiva, and the woolly mammoth mentioned in the tribal fable. I don't know about the Lightning Bird, but it definitely exists today in Africa. So does the marula tree, which bears fruit so alcoholic even elephants get drunk.

The reason several animals were woolly was the cold. Great ice sheets, three to five miles thick, surged forward and retreated, surged forward and retreated, changing both the terrain and the weather. It was the edge of such an ice sheet that Shiva saw in her vlsion.

That surge-retreat pattern persists, although the changes are so slow we do not notice them. We live at a time when Mamar has retreated, but only temporarily. Every scientist I know agrees the ice is coming back. Quite a few believe it could start coming back tomorrow.

The big cat with the saber teeth actually existed. It roamed through Europe for thousands of years, but died out before Shiva was born. If Shiva had lived in America, she might have seen Saber in the flesh instead of just finding his skull—that breed of tiger lasted longer in the New World than it did in the old.

The tribes to which Shiva belonged actually existed. They followed the herds of game in a constant migration, built rude shelters of branches and clay, and occasionally ventured into caves to paint. They used tools and weapons of flint, which they threw away when the

187

edges blunted. They worshipped a Mother Goddess, and there is every indication that the women ruled.

There is a notion about that prehistoric people spoke in grunts, like animals, but that is hard to believe. Their art was far from crude, and if their language was only half as rich, they could probably have talked as well as you or I.

The Weakling Strangers, as the ogres called them, are now referred to as Cro-Magnon people. They were tall and straight and clever. They were our ancestors.

—J. H. Brennan

Be sure not to miss the second book in J.B. Brennan's Ice Age trilogy, recently published by HarperCollins Publishers:

SHIVA ACCUSED

There was a body floating in the water.

Slender, outstretched arms had attracted a halo of thin ice, for ice still collected on the surface of the water hole overnight. The feet were pointed so that pale, callused flesh stared up at an overcast sky. The body itself faced down, gently bobbing on small ripples stirred by a chill wind from the morning sun.

Shiva watched from her vantage point upon the overhanging rock, her wolfskin drawn about her against the cold. She remained very silent and still.

There were two tawny cats on the far bank, one drinking unhurriedly, the other relaxed but alert, glancing about in no particular direction. Shiva took them for sisters from a hunting pride, or, just possibly, mother and daughter. They knew there was meat close by—the body floated only yards away—but she doubted they would try to retrieve it. Almost all the great cats hated water, and most lionesses preferred a fresh kill to carrion. Besides, they preferred horse or deer meat to human.

Wary of the cats, she approached the water hole to climb on the rock that overlooked the pool. She stared down and saw the cats; and with them, floating in the water hole, the body.

It seemed to be the body of a little man, short of stature with thin, elongated muscles. He was naked; nor was there sign of furs or skins nearby around the bank. Ritual scarring zig-zagged his upper back on a level with the shoulder blades, a little like the lodge marks of a warrior. Although she could not see his face, she knew he was not of her tribe, for the Shingu used dyes to mark its men, not scarring. Besides, she knew no warrior or hunter of his scrawny build.

Clearly he was dead, or if not dead then so close that it scarcely mattered. Besides, there was nothing she could do. Dead or alive, she would not venture closer to the water hole while the cats remained, not for a stranger.

Shiva waited. She wondered how the man

had died. None of the immediate possibilities seemed very likely. Had he come to wash, as she had, or to drink and then drowned? But how had he drowned? The water hole was not particularly deep, not deep at all near the edges where he would have washed or drunk. Even had he stumbled and fallen, he could have clambered out without much trouble.

Had he been seized by some powerful animal, savaged and killed? The lionesses would not have dragged him into the water. Nor did anything large enough to kill a man live in the water hole. Besides, what predator removed a man's clothing?

Spirits.

As the new thought occurred, Shiva shivered. The world was full of spirits—ancestral ghosts, visitations from the dreamtime, unnatural monsters temporarily made flesh. Had he been taken by the nightwing?

She stopped the questions and did something few of her tribe could do: she watched a picture in her mind. She had always felt different from her tribe. The pictures in her mind were an ogre trait, like the use of her left hand. All of her secret friends, ogres, could do it, did do it all the time—Doban and Thag and Hana and Dan and Heft the Hunter—but among her tribe, among humankind, the ability was rare. She was certain Hiram had it and possibly one small girl-child called Dawn. And the Crone.

The picture that formed in her mind was frightening, more frightening somehow than her earlier thoughts about the lioness's attack. It was a picture of darkness fitfully illuminated by an intermittent moon, of a slim, small figure moving through an area of rocky flatlands, made alien by night. She could not see the face, but the build made her certain it was the same person who now floated on the water.

Shiva watched this figure in her mind, moving with a brisk, surefooted gait that suggested an unusual familiarity with darkness. There was no fear in him, not of darkness, not of predators, not even of spirits, which were the greatest dangers of the night.

Yet there should have been fear, for suddenly, in her mind's eye, Shiva saw the wooden club smash down, crushing the forehead and part of the nose so that the features suddenly became a bloody pulp. She heard a short grunt, no more than that, no scream, no groan, for death came quickly.

Shiva shook her head. The picture in her mind was nonsense. Whatever the tribe, no warrior walked abroad at night. Not even men were so foolish as to take so great a risk of offending spirits and attracting the nightwing. Besides, the body floated in the water hole, drowned, not clubbed. It was still difficult to imagine how he might have drowned, but that was no excuse for wild imaginings.

One of the great cats moved away with feline grace. The other lingered for a moment, then followed. Shiva stood up and climbed down.

She waded in, and the level of the water was no higher than her waist when she caught the ankle of the floating warrior. He seemed older now than she had first imagined, far older than any warrior of her own tribe. Close to, the smell of death oozed from him like a cloud and she could see the body was misshapen, the spine twisted by age or the diseases of age, the fingers of the left hand clawlike from arthritis. But she drew it toward the bank in any case, holding her breath so that she would not accidentally suck the ancient spirit into her own body. The corpse floated easily, and even when she reached the bank she had little difficulty pulling it out, because it was so small and slight.

She hesitated then, prey to a sudden dread she could not understand. Death was no stranger to her, no stranger to any of the tribe. But this death disturbed her, even though the man was not of her tribe, not Shingu, thus none of her concern.

And yet she felt the dread.

Shiva glanced around, then turned him over. At once a chill hand seized her heart. He was not a man at all, but an old, old woman, wrinkled beyond belief. Her forehead and portion of her nose had been crushed, as if by a blow from a club.

• • •

Shiva was not sure what to do. Light though the body was as she had pulled it from the water, Shiva did not think she could carry it back to the Shingu encampment—nor could she decide if she should. The old woman was not of her tribe, no business of hers, no business of her tribe, so why try to bring her back to the camp, risking the possibility that her spirit would follow?

At the same time, she could not leave it here. Her nostrils told her that the cats were gone, but there would be other predators, less fastidious about carrion.

Shiva stared at the corpse, wondering who she had been. So old. So very old that it was almost impossible to believe any human being could have lived so long. What had she done, this old woman? Was she an elder of her tribe? Or just a favored grandmother who made herself useful by gathering nuts and grubs like the children? And what of the scarring on her back? That scar pattern had been placed there for a purpose, to mark her in some special way, as warriors were marked with paint when they were initiated into a lodge. Above all, how should Shiva deal with her body? Was it important? Did it matter?

The imaginary figure Shiva always called her mother (the mother who had died in childbirth giving Shiva life) appeared by her side unbidden. "It matters," Shiva's mother said; and disappeared again.

It mattered. Of course it mattered. Not because the woman was young or old. Not because she belonged to this tribe or that tribe. Not even because she was dead. It mattered because she had been murdered!

And there it was, the truth Shiva had striven to avoid, now hanging ominous and glittering in the forefront of her mind. What to do? She must hide the body, protect it somehow from the scavengers, then, when it was safe, she must run as fast as she could to the village camp and there tell Renka or some other elder. They would then decide what was to be done. Once she carried back the news, for Shiva the problem would be over.

She looked around. To keep a body safe from predators, even for a relatively short space of time, was not so easy as it sounded. What she needed, Shiva thought, was a rock cleft or small cave—something with a narrow entrance she could easily block off once the body was inside.

She looked around and noticed for the first

time a shadow (partly hidden by a bush) near the base of the rock on which she had lain to observe the cats. She approached it cautiously, half wondering, half hoping, and saw at once it might be what she needed. Behind the bush was an opening.

Shiva moved slowly, sniffing. It was difficult to judge the size of the cave from the outside. This entrance was narrow, but that signified little, for it might widen in the darkness within to create a den for bear or something else.

She was close to the opening now and there was no smell of cat, no smell of any animal. She took a deep breath and pushed the protective bush to one side. There was still no sound, still no hint of odor on the air. She dropped down on one knee, pushed forward and squeezed headfirst into the darkness.

Nothing seized her, nothing touched her. As her eyes grew accustomed to the gloom she saw she was in a cleft little more than eight feet deep, narrow and low, inhabited by nothing more destructive than a few sleepy spiders. It was perfect to protect the old woman's body.

Shiva wriggled out again. She stood up and trotted over to where the old one lay. She took one wrist, thin as a dried-up twig, to lift this frail little remnant across her shoulders ready to carry her the short distance to the cleft.

The old woman was even lighter than she

had imagined, weighing little more than a child. Shiva stumbled with the body spread across her shoulders, but recovered and carried it easily enough the short distance to the opening. Gently she set it down again, pushed the bush to one side and eased the body through the narrow opening.

As she did so, some sixth sense froze her into immobility. Slowly she straightened and looked behind her. Only yards away was a yellow-faced warrior in wolfskins, black feathers stuck into his hair, a fire-tempered spear in his right hand. Beside him was another, and another, and another ranged in a rough semicircle. Shiva's eyes flickered from one to the other. She was surrounded.

The warriors stared at her silently.

"Who are you?" Shiva asked at once, knowing enough to hide her fear. How had they come so close? No hint of their scent had reached her, no sound of their approach had pricked her ears. They were skilled, these warriors. She wondered to which of the tribes they belonged. She knew there were many other tribes, of course, but was too young to have had much direct experience of them and could not read the signs.

A woman pushed forward, dressed and painted like the men but without the feathers in her hair, obviously their leader. "I am

Weaver of the Barradik. What is your name and tribe, girl?" She had the sharp, confident tone of one accustomed to obedience. Perhaps she was an elder.

"I am Shiva, " Shiva said. "My tribe is the Shingu." She was about to add that their encampment was nearby, but thought better of it and was silent.

One of the men, a flat-faced fellow with a portion of his right ear missing, whispered something to the woman.

"What have you hidden in the cave, girl?" Weaver asked.

Shiva said nothing. She disliked the way the woman called her "girl" even after learning her name. She disliked the arrogance in the woman's tone and in the stance of the men.

The woman Weaver gestured and one of the men pushed Shiva brusquely to one side. He was too broad in the shoulder to squeeze through the cleft, but his eyes were keen enough to see despite the gloom. "Looks like a body in here, Weaver. Small body—a woman or a child. "

Weaver's eyes widened. "What is in there, girl?" Her tone, never pleasant, had taken on an icy edge of menace.

"An old woman," Shiva muttered sullenly.

"I can't hear you!" Weaver snapped .

"An old woman," Shiva repeated, more

loudly this time.

"Dead?"

"Yes."

"Why were you hiding her in the cave?" Weaver asked coldly .

Shiva lapsed back into silence. Some of her earlier fear was draining away, replaced by a growing anger. What right had this woman to question her? She was not even Shingu.

"Perhaps she murdered her," the flat-faced man suggested. He grinned .

"Did you kill her?" Weaver asked soberly. "Is that why you were trying to hide her in the cave? "

"No! " shouted Shiva, shocked.

"There's blood on her club," the flat-faced man remarked. His smile had dropped away, as if he was considering his own suggestion seriously for the first time.

Shiva looked down, her fear suddenly grown large again. "That's *jackal* blood!"

The warrior by the cleft reached in and began to pull the old woman's body out by one ankle.

"Maybe it is and maybe it isn't," said the flat-faced man, referring to Shiva's claim that the blood was jackal blood.

The body emerged into the light and Weaver stepped forward to inspect it. As she bent forward, Shiva heard the inadvertent gasp of horror.

"Mother Goddess!" Weaver exclaimed. Blood drained from her face. She stepped back so quickly she stumbled and would actually have fallen had not a warrior caught her arm.

"What's the matter, Weaver?" the man asked.

"It is the Hag!" Weaver gasped. "This girl has killed the Hag!"